THE ADVENTURES
of
PINOCCHIO

CARLO COLLODI

Translated by IAN PEDLOW

Ashton Scholastic. Sydney Auckland
New York   Toronto   London   Tokyo

First published in Seal Books 1974
Copyright © 1974 Ian Pedlow from the original Italian by
Carlo Collodi.
This edition is published by Ashton Scholastic by
arrangement with Rigby Limited.
National Library of Australia Card Number & ISBN
0 85179 098 4

Printed at The Griffin Press, Netley, Sth. Aust.

FOREWORD

Carlo Collodi was born at Florence, in Italy, in the year 1826, and he died there in 1890. His real name was Carlo Lorenzini. His pen-name, Collodi, was the name of the village from which his mother came.

Carlo was the oldest of ten children, and his parents were not very well off. He attended secondary school but, like Pinocchio, he was not a good student and was better known for his pranks than for his achievements.

His first job was in a library, but in 1848 he volunteered for the Tuscan Army. At that time Italy was not united under one government, and Tuscany, of which Florence was the capital, was one of a number of separate states. The Tuscans went to war to win freedom from their rulers, the Austrians, but they were not successful until many years later.

The war lasted a little over a year, and afterwards Collodi worked as a journalist and wrote plays and stories. From 1860 to 1881 he worked rather unwillingly as a clerk, first in the office of theatre censorship and then for the government of Florence. Throughout his life he kept on writing stories, mostly for children.

In 1880 he was asked to write a serial for "The Children's Magazine," and that is how Pinocchio came into existence. Since then it has been translated into most of the languages of the world.

Perhaps the reason for the continued popularity of Pinocchio is that every incident has a true moral— you can learn something by paying careful attention as you read. Also it is a very funny story, and Collodi himself had a humorous way of looking at life. When he was with his nephew on a steam train the little boy would keep on asking questions, such as, "Why does smoke come out of the engine?" Collodi would not answer at first, then he would say, "The engine smokes because it has had that bad habit since it was small, just as I have. It keeps on choofing like that because it is tired of always going on the same rail." Replies like this are just like some of the passages in Pinocchio.

In this translation I have left in a few Italian words to remind you that the story was written by an Italian. The pronunciation which is given is only approximate. If you know any Italians, you should ask them exactly how to say the words.

Even the word Pinocchio has a meaning: it means "pine seed," which is very suitable for a little boy of wood.

Ian Pedlow

How it happened that Master Ciliega, a carpenter, found a piece of wood that laughed and cried like a child.

Once upon a time there was a . . .

"A king!" my young readers will say at once.

No, children, you're wrong. Once upon a time there was a piece of wood.

It wasn't a special piece of wood. It was just an ordinary piece such as you might put in the stove in winter to start the fire and heat the rooms.

I don't know quite how, but one fine day this piece of wood was lying in the shop of an old carpenter whose name was Master Antonio. Everyone called him Master Ciliegia* because of the tip of his nose, which was always red and shiny like a ripe cherry.

Master Ciliegia was very pleased when he noticed the piece of wood. He rubbed his hands together happily, and said to himself:

"This piece of wood has turned up at just the right moment; I need it to make a leg for a table."

He picked up his sharp hatchet at once with the intention of cleaning off the bark and smoothing down the wood. But when he raised his arm for the first blow, he stopped with it hanging in the air because he heard a very small voice which pleaded:

"Don't hit me too hard!"

Just imagine the surprise of dear old Master Ciliegia!

*In Italian, Ciliegia means Cherry. It is pronounced "chee-lee-ay-ja."

1

He looked all around the room to see where that small voice could have come from, but saw no one. He looked under the bench: no one there. He looked in a cupboard that was always kept closed: no one there. He looked in the barrel of shavings and sawdust: no one there. He opened the door of the shop and looked up and down the street: no one there. Where had the voice come from?

"I know!" he said, laughing and rubbing his wig. "I must have imagined that small voice. Back to work!"

He picked up the hatchet again and brought it down with a hard whack on the piece of wood.

"Ouch! You have hurt me badly!" said the same small voice.

This time Master Ciliegia was even more surprised. His eyes were popping out with fright, his mouth fell open and his tongue was hanging almost down to his chin. His face looked like one carved on a fountain.

When he could speak again, he trembled and stuttered with fear:

"Where did the little voice come from that said 'Ouch'? There's not a living soul here. Could it be that somehow this piece of wood has learnt to cry out like a child? I can't believe it. This is just a piece of firewood like all the rest; I could throw it in the fire to heat up a saucepan of beans . . . Then where did the voice come from? Could there be someone hidden in the wood? If there is, so much the worse for him! I'll make him welcome!"

And he took that poor piece of wood in both hands and began knocking it against the wall without mercy.

Then he stopped to listen, to see if there were any complaints from the small voice. He waited two minutes, and heard nothing; five minutes, and nothing; ten minutes, and still nothing.

"I know!" he said, forcing himself to laugh and running his hand through his wig, "I have imagined that small voice that said 'Ouch.' Back to work."

2

But because he was really very afraid, he began to hum a tune to make him feel brave.

Then he picked up his plane to clean and smooth the piece of wood, but while he was planing back and forth he heard the same small voice say laughingly:

"Stop it! You're tickling me all over!"

This time poor Master Ciliegia fell down as though struck by lightning. When he opened his eyes again, he found himself sitting on the floor.

He looked very frightened, and even the point of his nose had changed from its usual red to a dark blue colour.

CHAPTER 2

Master Ciliega presents the piece of wood to his friend Geppetto, who intends to make himself a wonderful puppet that can dance, fight with a sword and turn somersaults.

At this moment there was a knock at the door.

"Come in," said the carpenter, who had not even the strength to lift himself off the floor.

A sprightly old man entered the shop. His name was Geppetto, but the children of the neighbourhood, when they wanted to get his temper up, used to call him by the nickname of "Polendina"* because of his yellow wig which looked just like maize pudding.

Geppetto was very quick tempered. If anyone called him "Polendina" he became as angry as a wild bull and it was impossible to calm him down.

"Good morning, Master Antonio," said Geppetto. "What are you doing there on the ground?"

"I am teaching arithmetic to the ants."

"A lot of good that will do you!"

"What has brought you to see me, my dear Geppetto?"

"My legs have brought me. To tell the truth, Master Antonio, I have come to ask you a favour."

"Well here I am, ready to help you," answered the carpenter, getting up onto his knees.

"This morning I was suddenly struck by a good idea."

"Let me hear it."

"I thought of making myself a beautiful wooden puppet, a wonderful puppet that can dance, fight with a

*This would be like calling someone "Pudding Head" in English.

4

sword, and turn somersaults. I intend to travel the world with this puppet, earning my keep as I go. What do you think of the idea?"

"Clever Polendina!" cried the same small voice that seemed to come from nowhere.

When he heard himself called Polendina, Geppetto turned red with anger and rushed at the carpenter.

"Why do you insult me?" he shouted.

"Who is insulting you?"

"You called me Polendina."

"It wasn't me."

"Next you'll say that I said it myself! It *was* you!"

"No!"

"Yes!"

"No!"

"Yes!"

They became more and more excited until they were hitting, scratching, and biting one another.

When the fight was over, Master Antonio found Geppetto's yellow wig in his hands, and Geppetto had the carpenter's grey wig in his mouth.

"Give me back my wig," said Master Antonio.

"And you return mine, and let us be friends again."

The two old men put their own wigs back on, shook hands, and promised to remain good friends for the rest of their lives.

"Now, my dear Geppetto," the carpenter said in a friendly voice, "what is it that I can do for you?"

"I should like a piece of wood to make my puppet. Could you please give me one?"

Master Antonio went happily to the bench to get the piece of wood that had frightened him so badly. But when he was handing it to his friend it gave a sharp jerk, wriggled out of his hand, and beat itself sharply against the weak old shins of poor Geppetto.

"Well Master Antonio! Is this the kindness with which you offer me a gift! You've almost made me lame."

"I swear that I did not do it!"

5

"Then it was me?"

"It is all the fault of this wood . . ."

"I know all about the wood, but you're the one who hit me on the legs with it!"

"I did not hit you!"

"Liar!"

"Geppetto, do not insult me, or I will call you Polendina!"

"Ass!"

"Polendina!"

"Donkey!"

"Polendina!"

"Ugly ape!"

"Polendina!"

On hearing himself called Polendina for the third time, Geppetto went blind with rage. He threw himself at the carpenter and they fought fiercely.

At the end of the battle Master Antonio found that he had two more scratches on his nose, and Geppetto had two less buttons on his coat. When they had settled their differences in this way, they shook hands and promised to remain good friends for the rest of their lives.

Geppetto picked up his fine piece of wood, thanked Master Antonio, and returned home with a limp.

7

Geppetto returns home and starts at once to make his puppet, which he calls Pinocchio. The puppet is soon up to mischief.

Geppetto lived in a small room on the ground floor which received its light from beneath a stairway. The furniture was very simple—one battered chair, a bed not much better, and a half-broken little table. Low down on the wall you could see a stove with a fire alight, but the fire was only painted there, and beside the fire there was painted a saucepan which boiled cheerfully and sent out a cloud of steam, which looked quite real.

As soon as he reached home Geppetto took out his tools and began to carve out his puppet and put the pieces together.

"What name shall I give it?" he asked himself. "I'll call it Pinocchio. That name will bring it good luck. I once knew a whole family of Pinocchios: father Pinocchio, mother Pinocchio, and all the little Pinocchios. They all got along so well that the richest of them was a beggar!"

Once he had named his puppet he was able to work more quickly. He made the hair, the forehead, and the eyes.

You can imagine his surprise when the eyes moved around and then stared hard at him!

Geppetto did not like to have those wooden eyes fixed on him, and said in a hurt voice:

8

"Little eyes of wood, why are you staring at me?"

No answer came.

Next he made the nose, but this was no sooner completed than it began to grow, and grow, and grow, so that in a few minutes there seemed to be no end to it.

Poor Geppetto was soon tired from cutting it back, but the more that he cut and trimmed it, the longer that cheeky nose grew.

Next he made the mouth.

No sooner had he finished than it began to laugh and sing.

"Stop laughing!" said Geppetto, who was annoyed, but he might as well have spoken to the wall.

"Stop laughing, I said!" he shouted loudly.

Then the mouth stopped laughing, but the tongue shot out.

Geppetto did not want to spoil his work, so he took no notice and kept on with the job. He made the chin, the neck, the shoulders, the stomach, the arms, and the legs.

When the hands were done, Geppetto felt his wig rising off his head. And what do you think he saw when he turned around? He saw the yellow wig in the puppet's hand.

"Pinocchio! Give me back my wig at once."

And Pinocchio, instead of returning the wig, put it on his own head and tried hard not to laugh.

This naughty and rude behaviour made Geppetto more sad and disappointed than he had ever been before. He came close to Pinocchio and said, "You rascal of a boy! You begin to show a lack of respect for your father even before I've finished making you. You're a very naughty boy!"

He dried a tear from his eye, and began to make the legs and feet. No sooner had he finished than he felt a kick on the end of his nose.

"I deserve it," he said to himself. "I should have thought of it before. Now it is too late."

Then he picked up the puppet and put it on the floor to see if it could walk. Pinocchio's legs were still stiff and he did not know how to move them, so Geppetto took him by the hand and taught him how to put one foot after the other.

When the legs loosened up Pinocchio began to walk by himself, and then to run around the room. Before long he went through the door, jumped into the street, and began to run away.

Poor Geppetto ran after him but could not catch him because that rascal of a Pinocchio went jumping along like a hare, his feet beating on the paving stones and making a noise like the boots of twenty farmers.

"Catch him! Catch him!" cried Geppetto, but the people in the street just stood and looked in amazement at this wooden thing that ran as fast as a racehorse. They could not stop laughing at the strange sight.

At last, by good luck, a policeman arrived on the scene. He had heard the uproar and thought that it must be a young horse that had escaped from its owner. The policeman placed himself bravely in the middle of the road, with his legs apart, determined to stop the foal before there was a serious accident.

When Pinocchio saw the policeman blocking the road he tried to take him by surprise and get past him by diving between his legs, but he didn't stand a chance.

Without moving an inch, the policeman seized him cleanly by the nose (that enormous nose seemed to have been made for policemen to catch hold of) and delivered him into the hands of Geppetto. Geppetto intended to punish him at once by boxing his ears soundly and was surprised when he could not find any ears. And do you know why? In his hurry to finish making the puppet, Geppetto had forgotten to give him ears.

He took Pinocchio by the scruff of the neck and led him along the street.

"Home we go!" he said. "Then you'll get what you deserve!"

When Pinocchio heard this warning he threw himself on the ground and refused to move. A crowd of people gathered around.

"Poor little puppet!" said one.

"He's got good reason for not wanting to return home!" said another.

"Who knows what that brute of a Geppetto might do to him!" said someone else.

And others joined in and said in a nasty tone: "That Geppetto pretends to be a good man, but he's a big bully! If he gets that poor little puppet in his hands, he's capable of tearing it to pieces! . . ."

The crowd made such a noise and fuss that the policeman let Pinocchio free again and took poor Geppetto to prison. Geppetto was so upset that he could not think what to say to save himself, and he cried like a baby. "My unhappy child!" he cried. "And to think that I have been to so much trouble to make it a good puppet! But it serves me right! I should have known before! . . ."

What happened afterwards is a story that you will scarcely be able to believe. I shall tell it in the next chapter.

CHAPTER 4

The story of Pinocchio and the Talking Cricket, in which we see how naughty children do not like to be corrected by those who know better than they do.

Poor Geppetto, who had done nothing wrong, was taken to jail, and that young rascal Pinocchio, who was set free by the policeman, ran off across the fields as fast as his legs would carry him. He headed straight for home, and in his great hurry he jumped over steep slopes, thorny hedges, and ditches full of water, like a kid goat or a young hare chased by a hunter.

He found the door of the house partly open. He went in, closed and bolted the door behind him, threw himself on the ground, and heaved a deep sigh of happiness.

But his happiness did not last long, because he heard someone in the room say:

"Cri, cri, cri!"

"Who's that calling me?" said Pinocchio, very much afraid.

"It's me!"

Pinocchio turned and saw a large cricket which was climbing slowly up the wall.

"Who are you, cricket?"

"I am the Talking Cricket, and I've been living in this room for more than a hundred years."

"Today, however, this room is mine," said the puppet, "and you would do me a great favour by going away at once, without even turning around."

"I shall not leave here," answered the cricket,

"before telling you an important truth."

"Tell me, and leave quickly!"

"Woe to those children who rebel against their parents and take it into their head to run away from home. They will never have luck in this world, and sooner or later they will be very sorry for what they've done."

"Keep on singing just as you like, Mister Cricket. As for me, tomorrow at dawn I intend to go away from here, because if I stay the same will happen to me as to all other children. I shall be sent to school and made to study whether I want to or not. And let me tell you, just between the two of us, that I have no desire at all to study. All I want to do is to chase after butterflies and climb trees to take little birds from their nests."

"You poor fool! Can't you see that if you carry on in that way you will grow up to be a silly creature and everyone will make fun of you?"

"Shut up, Mister Cricket! Don't say those nasty things about me."

The cricket, who was patient and thoughtful, was not upset by this rudeness; he went on in the same tone of voice, "If you don't think you'll enjoy school, then why not learn a trade so that you'll be able to earn an honest living?"

"Do you want me to tell you?" replied Pinocchio, who was beginning to lose his patience. "Among all the trades of the world there is only one that I really like."

"And what trade is that?"

"The trade of eating, drinking, sleeping, enjoying myself, and leading the life of a vagabond from morning to night."

"For your information," said the Talking Cricket calmly, "anyone who follows that trade nearly always finishes up in hospital or in prison."

"Watch yourself, Mister Cricket! Don't say those nasty things about me. If I lose my temper, it will be bad luck for you!"

14

"Poor Pinocchio! I am really sorry for you."

"Why are you sorry for me?"

"Because you are a puppet and, which is worse, you have a head of wood."

At this last word Pinocchio jumped up in a fury, grabbed a hammer from the bench, and threw it at the Talking Cricket. Perhaps he did not even mean to hit it, but unfortunately he caught it right on the head. The poor cricket hardly had time to say "Cri cri cri" before he was stuck on the wall quite dead.

CHAPTER

Pinocchio feels hungry, and breaks an egg to poach it. But before long the poached egg flies away out of the window.

Meanwhile night was coming on and Pinocchio, remembering that he had eaten nothing, heard in his stomach a little rumbling that sounded just like a slightly hungry feeling. But in children such a feeling grows quickly. In a few minutes he was very hungry, and before long he believed that he was starving.

Little Pinocchio ran towards the fireplace, where there was a boiling saucepan, and put his hand out to take off the lid and see what was inside. But the saucepan was painted on the wall. You can imagine how surprised he was! His nose, which was already long, grew at least another four inches.

He raced around the room, hunting through boxes and poking into hiding places, searching for a piece of old bread, a crust, a dog's bone, a mouldy pudding, the backbone of a fish, the stone of a cherry, anything that he could bite on. But he found nothing, nothing at all.

All the time his hunger was growing worse. Poor Pinocchio had no relief except swallowing, and sometimes he gave such a big swallow, just like a yawn, that his mouth nearly reached his ears. Then he spat, and he felt as though his stomach had come out of his mouth.

"The Talking Cricket was right," he said, crying hopelessly. "I have been bad to revolt against my father and run away from the house. If my father were

16

here now, I wouldn't be half dead with hunger. Oh, hunger is a terrible thing!"

Next moment he noticed something round and white on top of a little pile of rubbish. It looked like a hen's egg. He gave a jump and was beside it at once. It really was an egg.

The joy of the little puppet was too much for words. He thought he was dreaming; he turned the egg over and over in his hands; he even kissed it.

"Now how shall I cook it?" he asked himself. "Shall I make an omelette? No, it will be better poached! . . . But perhaps it might be tastier if I fry it in a pan? Or if I make a drink out of it? No, it will be quickest to poach it or fry it. I'm in such a hurry to eat it!"

It was no sooner said than done. He placed the frying pan on a little stove full of burning wood. Instead of oil or butter, he put water in the pan, and when the water began to boil he cracked the shell of the egg so as to slide it into the pan.

It was not yolk and white that came out of the egg, but a little chicken. The little bird was very happy and grateful, and bowed gracefully before saying, "A thousand thanks to you, Mister Pinocchio, for saving me the trouble of breaking the shell. My best wishes to all in this house. Farewell and goodbye!"

Then he spread his wings, flew through the open window, and was gone in a moment.

The poor little puppet just stood and stared like someone under a spell, with eyes fixed, mouth open, and the egg-shell in his hands. When he got over his first surprise he began to cry, scream, and stamp his feet. He said between his cries, "The Talking Cricket was right! If I had not run away from home, and if my father were still here, I wouldn't find myself dying of hunger."

His stomach longed for food more than ever, and as he could not satisfy it he thought of leaving the house to make a quick visit to the near-by village. He hoped to find a kind person who would give him a little bread.

CHAPTER 6

Pinocchio falls asleep with his feet on the heater, and wakes up next morning with his feet badly burnt.

It was a cold, wet night. The thunder roared and the lightning flashed as though the sky were going to catch on fire. The wind blew violently, and made a shrieking noise and raised a huge cloud of dust. All the trees creaked and groaned.

Pinocchio was very frightened of the thunder and lightning, but his hunger was greater than his fear, and this made him set out on his way. He ran and jumped along at a great rate, soon reaching the near-by village. His tongue was hanging out and his breath came in pants, like a tired dog.

The village was dark and empty. The windows were closed and in the street not even a dog was to be seen.

Pinocchio, who was very hungry and scared, rang loudly on the bell of a house, saying to himself: "Someone must come!"

An old man in a nightcap opened a window and said angrily,

"What do you want at this hour?"

"I wonder would you be good enough to give me a little piece of bread?"

"Wait there for me. I'll be back in a minute," said the old man, who believed that he was dealing with one of those naughty boys who amuse themselves at night by

18

ringing the bells on houses just for the sake of annoying people who are fast asleep.

In a few minutes the window opened again and the old man called to Pinocchio,

"Stand under the window and have your hat ready."

Pinocchio, who did not have a hat, moved under the window. He soon felt water pouring over him from an enormous basin. He was soaked from head to foot, as though a vase of withered geraniums had been tipped over him.

He returned home like a wet chicken, exhausted and hungry. He was too weak to stand any longer. He flopped down and leant his wet muddy feet against a stove full of hot coals.

There he fell asleep, and while he slept his feet, being made of wood, began to smoulder, and slowly went black and turned to ashes.

Pinocchio just kept on sleeping and snoring, as if the feet belonged to someone else. He did not wake up until daybreak, when someone knocked on the door.

"Who is it?" he called, yawning and rubbing his eyes.

"It's me," a voice answered.

That was Geppetto's voice.

CHAPTER 7

Geppetto returns home, and gives the puppet the breakfast that he had brought for himself.

Poor Pinocchio, who was half asleep, had not yet noticed that his feet were burnt off. As soon as he heard his father's voice he slid from his stool to run and open the bolt on the door, but after a couple of stumbling steps he fell heavily on the floor and lay there stretched out. In falling he made a noise like a sack full of wooden spoons falling from the fifth floor.

"Let me in!" Geppetto shouted from the street.

"I can't, daddy," the puppet answered, crying while he tumbled about on the floor.

"Why can't you?"

"Because he's eaten my feet off."

"Who has eaten them off?" asked Geppetto.

"The cat," said Pinocchio. He had just seen the cat amusing itself by knocking some chips of wood along with its paws.

"Let me in, I say!" repeated Geppetto. "Otherwise I'll give you 'cat' when I get in!"

"Believe me, I cannot stand up! Oh, now I shall have to walk on my knees for the rest of my life."

Geppetto believed that these wailing noises were more of the puppet's mischief, and was determined to put an end to them. He climbed into the room through the window.

He knew just what he wanted to do, but when he saw

Pinocchio lying on the floor with his feet really gone, his anger disappeared. He picked up the puppet in his arms, kissed and stroked him gently, and said all sorts of soothing things. Large tear drops fell down his beard, and he said with a sob, "My dear little Pinocchio, how did your feet come to be burnt off?"

"I don't know, daddy, but I can tell you that it has been a terrible winter's night and that all I can remember is being out in it. The thunder roared and the lightning flashed and I was very hungry, and the Talking Cricket said to me, 'It serves you right. You have been naughty and you deserve it,' and I said, 'Be careful, Mister Cricket,' and he said, 'You are a puppet and you have a wooden head,' and I threw a hammer and killed him, but it was his fault, because I did not mean to kill him, and after that I put a pan on the stove, but the chicken escaped out of it and said, 'Farewell, and best wishes to all in this house,' and my hunger was getting worse all the time, for which reason that old man with the nightcap came to the window and said to me, 'Stand under the window and have your hat ready,' and I received a basinful of water on my head, because asking for a little bread is nothing to be ashamed of, is it? I came home immediately, and because I was still very hungry I put my feet on the stove to dry myself, and you returned, and I found them burnt off, and I'm still hungry and I haven't any feet! Oh! Oh! Oh!"

And poor Pinocchio began to cry and yell so loudly that he was heard five miles away.

From all that mixed-up speech Geppetto had understood only one thing, which was that the puppet felt as though he were dying of hunger. He took three pears from his pocket, handed them to Pinocchio, and said, "These were for my breakfast, but I give them to you gladly. Eat them. They will make you feel better."

"If you want me to eat them, please peel them first."

"Peel them?" replied Geppetto with astonishment

"I would never have thought that you were so fussy and hard to please about food. It's a pity. In this life, even when we're children, we must become accustomed to eating whenever food is offered to us, and we should learn to eat all kinds of things, because we never know what might happen to us. You must always remember that!"

"I'm sure that's true," answered Pinocchio, "but I never eat fruit that has not been peeled. I cannot bear to eat peel."

So the good Geppetto took out a little knife and patiently peeled the three pears and placed the peel on the corner of the table.

When Pinocchio had finished the first pear he tried to throw away the core, but Geppetto held his arm and said,

"Don't throw it away; in this life there is a use for everything."

"But I certainly cannot eat the core!" cried the puppet, turning on him like a snake.

"Who can say? You must remember that," replied Geppetto, without getting excited.

The three cores were saved from being thrown out of the window, and were placed on the corner of the table beside the peel.

When he had eaten, or rather devoured, the three pears, Pinocchio gave a big yawn and said with a loud sob,

"I'm still hungry."

"Well, my boy, I have nothing else to give you."

"Nothing at all?"

"Only this peel and these three cores."

"Oh well," said Pinocchio, "if there's nothing else I'll eat some peel," and he began to chew on it.

At first he pulled a face, but then, quite quickly, he cleaned up the bits of peel one after the other, and after the peel, down went the cores. Then he patted his hands contentedly on his stomach, and said, "Now I am really full!"

"You can see now," Geppetto remarked, "that I was right when I told you that we must not be too fussy and hard to please about food. My dear boy, in this life we never know what might happen to us. You must remember that!"

The puppet had no sooner satisfied his hunger than he began to grumble and cry because he wanted a new pair of feet.

But Geppetto let him cry and complain for half the day as a way of punishing him for the mischief he had done. Then he said,

"Why should I make you another pair of feet? Just for the sake of seeing you run away from home again?"

"I promise," the puppet sobbed, "that from now on I shall be good."

"That is what all children say when they want something."

"I promise that I will go to school and study and you'll be proud of me."

"All children have the same story when they want something."

"But I am not like the others. I am better than other boys and I always tell the truth. I promise you, daddy, that I'll learn a trade and look after you in your old age, and you'll be proud of me."

Although Geppetto was a stern man, his eyes filled with tears and his heart was full of pity at the sad sight of Pinocchio. Without speaking a word he picked up his wood-carving tools and two small pieces of dry, hard wood and set to work.

In less than an hour the two feet were completed: two neat little feet, slim and strong, that were the work of an artist of genius.

Then Geppetto said to the puppet, "Close your eyes and go to sleep," and Pinocchio closed his eyes and pretended to sleep.

Geppetto used a little soft glue, held in an eggshell, to stick the two feet in place, and he did this so skilfully that no one could have seen the join.

No sooner was the puppet aware of having his feet than he jumped down from the table where he had been lying and began to frisk and caper about as if he were mad with happiness.

"I should like to go to school at once to repay you for what you have done for me," Pinocchio said to his father.

"Good boy!"

"But before I go to school I shall need a few clothes."

Geppetto, who was poor, did not even have a single cent in his pocket, so he made Pinocchio a little suit out of paper with flowers printed on it, a pair of shoes from the bark of a tree, and a little hat from a crust of bread.

Pinocchio ran quickly to look at his reflection in a bowl of water, and was so pleased with his appearance that he said proudly, "I look like a real gentleman!"

"That's right," replied Geppetto. "You must remember that it is not fine clothes that make a gentleman, but clean clothes."

"It seems to me," said Pinocchio, "that something else is always needed for school. The main thing is still missing."

"What is that?"

"I need a reader."

"Yes, but how are we to get one?"

"That's simple. You go to a bookshop and buy one."

"And the money?"

"I haven't got it."

"Nor have I," the kind old man added sadly.

And Pinocchio, who was usually a happy boy, was sad too, because some sadness is felt by everyone, even little boys.

"Wait!" cried Geppetto, getting up suddenly and taking off his old corduroy coat which was all patched and mended. He ran out of the house.

In a short time he returned with a school reader in his hand, but he no longer had his coat. The poor man was in his shirt sleeves, and outside it was snowing.

"Where is your coat, daddy?"

"I sold it."

"Why did you sell it?"

"Because I felt hot."

Pinocchio understood this reply at once and, unable to restrain the swelling of his good heart, he threw his arms around Geppetto's neck and kissed him many times.

CHAPTER 9

Pinocchio sells his school reader so that he can go to see a puppet play.

When the snow had stopped falling Pinocchio set off for school with his beautiful new reader under his arm. As he went along he made up many wonderful stories about himself and built lots of fine castles in the air.

He said to himself, "Today at school I shall learn at once to read and write. Tomorrow I shall learn arithmetic. Then, because I am so clever, I shall earn lots of money, and the first thing I do will be to buy a beautiful woollen coat for my daddy. But why woollen? I'll get one of gold and silver, with pearls for buttons. And that poor man certainly deserves it. He bought my book and made me learn, and to make it possible he has left himself in shirt sleeves in this freezing weather. There aren't many fathers who are capable of such sacrifices."

Just then he seemed to hear in the distance the music of pipes and drums: tum, ti-tum, ti-tum. He stopped to listen. The sounds came from the bottom of a long crossroad which led to a small township built on the seashore.

"What can the music be? What a pity that I must go to school; but for that . . . ."

He hesitated. Well, he must make up his mind one way or the other: to school, or to hear the pipes and drums?

"Today I'll go to hear the music, and tomorrow to

28

school. There is always time for school," said the little rascal with a shrug of his shoulders.

Next moment he was running down the crossroad. The more he ran, the clearer was the sound of pipes and the thud of the drums: tum, ti-tum, ti-tum, tum, tum.

He soon found himself in a square full of people who were crowding around a large tent painted with bright colours.

"What's the tent for?" asked Pinocchio, turning to a young lad near by.

"Read the sign there, and then you'll know."

"I'd read it gladly, but just for today I cannot read."

"Clever fellow! Then I'll read it for you. That sign says, in letters as red as flame,

'THE GREAT PUPPET THEATRE'."

"Is it long since the show started?"

"It's starting now."

"How much does it cost to get in?"

"Ten cents."

Now Pinocchio could think only of seeing the puppet theatre and had forgotten all his good resolutions. He said boldly to the boy,

"Will you lend me ten cents until tomorrow?"

"I'd lend it to you gladly," said the boy jokingly, "but just for today I'm afraid I can't manage it."

"I'll sell you my coat for ten cents," said the little puppet.

"What do you think I could do with a coat of flowered paper? If it rained, I couldn't get it off my back."

"Do you want to buy my shoes?"

"They would be useful only for lighting the fire."

"How much will you give me for my hat?"

"A lot of use that would be! A hat made from old bread! The mice would probably come and eat it.

Pinocchio could think of only one more thing. He tried to make a last offer, but his courage failed him. He hesitated but at last managed to say, "Will you give me ten cents for this new reader?"

"I make a rule of not buying from other boys," said the young lad, who had much more sense than Pinocchio.

"I'll buy the reader for ten cents," cried a secondhand dealer who had overheard the conversation. And the book changed hands at once.

Meanwhile poor Geppetto was at home, shivering in his shirtsleeves, because he had bought the reader for his son.

CHAPTER 10

The puppets recognize their brother Pinocchio and welcome him joyfully. However the puppeteer Mangiafoco* appears, and Pinocchio seems likely to come to a nasty end.

When Pinocchio entered the little puppet theatre something happened that nearly led to a riot. First of all, however, I must tell you that the curtains had been lifted and the show had already started.

On the stage, Arlecchino and Pulcinella** were acting out a quarrel, as is usual in puppet plays, and threatening at each moment to let go at one another with smacks and blows.

The audience was following the play closely. The people were nearly bursting their sides with laughter at the argument between the two puppets, who were nodding and waving their arms at one another just like two real people.

All of a sudden Arlecchino stopped reciting, turned towards the audience, and pointed with his finger towards someone sitting in the theatre. He cried out in a dramatic voice:

"Heavens above! Am I dreaming? That's Pinocchio down there!"

"It certainly is Pinocchio!" shouted Pulcinella.

"No doubt about it!" screeched Mrs Rosaura, peeping up from below the stage.

*Mangiafoco means "fire eater" in Italian. It is pronounced "Man-jar-fo-ko."
**In English we would call them Punch and Judy. The Italian words are pronounced "Are-lek-key-no" and "Pul-chi-nel-la."

"It's Pinocchio! It's Pinocchio!" the puppets cried out in chorus, jumping into sight five at a time. Our brother Pinocchio! Hurrah for Pinocchio!"

"Pinocchio, come up here to me!" shouted Arlecchino. "Come and throw yourself into the arms of your brothers made of wood!"

When he heard this friendly greeting, he jumped from the back seats to the front, then with another jump landed on the head of the orchestra leader, and hopped from there onto the stage.

It is impossible to describe the embraces, the hugs, the loving squeezes, the knocking together of heads in true and sincere friendship, that Pinocchio received from the wooden actors and actresses in the middle of the great confusion.

They made a very touching sight, but when the audience found that the play was not to continue they became impatient and began to cry out, "We want the play! We want the play!"

It was a waste of breath. Instead of going on with the play, the puppets redoubled the shouting and uproar and, placing Pinocchio on their shoulders, carried him in triumph to the front of the footlights.

Then the puppeteer came forward. He was so big and ugly that people were frightened just by looking at him. He had a huge beard, as black as Indian ink, and so long that it stretched from his chin to the floor. It got under his feet when he walked. His mouth was as large as a furnace, his eyes looked like two bright red lanterns, and he carried a large whip made of snakes' and wolves' tails twisted together, which he cracked as he walked.

Everyone stopped breathing when he appeared. You could have heard a pin drop. The poor little puppets were trembling like leaves.

"Why have you come to throw my theatre into confusion?" the puppeteer asked Pinocchio, with a voice like an ogre who had a bad cold in the head.

"Believe me, sir, it is not my fault!"

"Enough! We'll see about you this evening."

When the play was finished the puppeteer went to the kitchen where he was preparing a fine leg of mutton for dinner. It was burning slowly on a spit over the fire. He did not have enough wood to finish the cooking, so he called Arlecchino and Pulcinella and said:

"Bring me that puppet who's tied to the nail. He seems to be made of well-dried wood, and I'm sure that if I throw him on the fire he'll burn very well for browning the roast."

Arlecchino and Pulcinella hesitated at first, but one stern look from their master made them obey. They soon returned carrying the poor Pinocchio who was wriggling like an eel out of water. He cried out with fright, "Save me, daddy! I don't want to die! I don't want to die!"

CHAPTER 11

Mangiafoco sneezes and pardons Pinocchio, who then saves from death his friend Arlecchino.

Mangiafoco was terrifying to look at, with his black beard that covered his body and legs like an apron. But he was not really a bad man, and he proved this when Pinocchio was brought to him. The poor little puppet was turning this way and that and crying, "I don't want to die! I don't want to die!" Mangiafoco began to soften and feel pity at once. At first he did not show his feelings, but before very long he gave a loud sneeze.

Until that moment Arlecchino was sad because of Pinocchio and had let himself slip into a bent position like a weeping willow tree. Now he cheered up quickly, and whispered quietly to Pinocchio: "Good news, brother. The puppeteer's sneeze is a sign that he has grown kinder and feels sorry for you. You will be safe."

My young readers must know that some people show pity for another by crying, or at least pretending to dry their eyes. Mangiafoco was different however, because whenever he had tender feelings he could not help sneezing. It was his way of letting others know the feelings of his heart.

After sneezing the puppeteer still kept up his show of a gruff manner by shouting at Pinocchio. "Stop crying! Your howling has given me a pain right here in the bottom of the stomach. I feel almost . . . ahh . . . choo, ahh . . . choo," and he sneezed twice more.

"Bless you!" said Pinocchio.

"Thank you. Are your mother and father still alive?" Mangiafoco asked.

"My father is alive, but I have never known my mother."

"Alas! How unhappy your father will be if I throw you into these burning ashes. Poor old man! I feel sorry for him! . . . Ahh . . . choo, ahh . . .choo, ahh . . . choo," and he sneezed three more times.

"Bless you!" said Pinocchio.

"Thank you. On the other hand, I am to be pitied also because, as you see, I have no more wood for cooking this roast mutton, and, to tell you the truth, you would have served my needs perfectly! But now I am feeling kinder and am inclined to let you off. Instead of you, I shall choose one of my own puppets to burn under the spit . . . Hi there, come along you policemen!"

At this command, two wooden policemen suddenly appeared. They were very tall and very dry, with feathered hats on their heads and swords in their hands.

The puppeteer said in a rumbling voice, "Fetch Arlecchino here, tie him up securely, and throw him on the fire. I want my mutton well roasted."

You can imagine how afraid poor Arlecchino was! His legs collapsed beneath him and he fell face first on the floor. This sad sight caused Pinocchio to throw himself at the feet of the puppeteer and to cry so much that his tears flowed onto the long black beard.

"Have pity, Mister Mangiafoco!" he pleaded.

"There are no 'Misters' here!" the puppeteer replied harshly.

"Have pity, good Knight!"

"There are no Knights here!"

"Have pity, Commander!"

"There are no Commanders here!"

"Have pity, Your Excellency!"

At the name Excellency the puppeteer did not shout

back. He immediately became more calm and reasonable. "What do you want from me?" he asked.

"Please pardon poor Arlecchino."

"Pardon does not apply in this case. If I spare you, it is necessary to make a fire out of him, because I want my mutton well roasted."

"If that is so," Pinocchio shouted proudly, standing up and throwing away his cap of stale bread, "if that is so then I know my duty. Forward, policemen! Tie me up and throw me into the flames. It is not right that poor Arlecchino, my good friend, should die for me!"

These words, spoken in a loud, brave voice, made all the puppets cry. Even the wooden policemen cried like two babies.

At first Mangiafoco remained hard and cold like a block of ice, and then, slowly, even he was moved and began to sneeze. After four or five sneezes, he opened his arms affectionately and said to Pinocchio,

"You are a good, brave boy! Come here and give me a kiss."

Pinocchio ran to him at once, climbed up his beard like a squirrel, and placed a beautiful kiss right on the end of his nose.

"Is the pardon granted then?" asked poor Arlecchino, his voice so quiet that it could hardly be heard.

"The pardon is granted," answered Mangiafoco, and he added, sighing and shaking his head, "For this evening I shall resign myself to eating half-cooked mutton, but another time, watch out for the one whose turn it is!"

As soon as they were sure of the pardon the puppets ran all over the stage and lit the candles and lamps as though it were an evening performance. They began leaping about and dancing, and when dawn came they were still dancing.

CHAPTER 12

Mangiafoco gives Pinocchio five pieces of gold for his father, Geppetto. Pinocchio, on his way home, lets himself be tricked by a fox and a cat and goes away with them.

Next day Mangiafoco called Pinocchio aside and asked him,

"What is your father's name?"

"Geppetto."

"And what is his trade?"

"Poverty."

"Does he earn much at it?"

"He earns so much that he never has a cent in his pocket. Would you believe that he was forced to sell his only coat in order to buy me a school reader, and it was a coat so full of patches and mends that it was a sight for sore eyes."

"Poor devil! I'm almost sorry for him. Here are five gold coins. Go at once and give them to him, with good wishes from me."

You can imagine how Pinocchio thanked the puppeteer over and over again. Then he gave a hug to each of the puppets in turn, even the policemen. And at last he set off for home feeling very pleased with himself.

He had gone only half a mile when he met on the road a fox with one lame foot and a cat blind in both eyes. These two friends in misfortune were trudging along steadily, one helping the other. The lame fox leant against the cat, and the blind cat was led by the fox.

"Good morning, Pinocchio," said the fox politely.

"How do you know my name?" asked the puppet.

"I know your father well."

"Where have you seen him?"

"I saw him yesterday at the door of his house."

"And what was he doing?"

"He was in shirt sleeves and shivering with cold."

"Poor daddy! But, God willing, he won't shiver any more after today."

"Why not?"

"Because I have become an important person."

"You an important person!" said the fox, and laughed rather unpleasantly. The cat laughed too, but held his paws up to his whiskers so that it would not be noticed.

"There's nothing to laugh at," cried Pinocchio with annoyance. "It gives me no pleasure to make your mouth water, but I can show you, if you care to look, five beautiful gold coins."

And he held out the money that Mangiafoco had given him.

At the pleasant tinkle of that money, the fox stretched out the leg that appeared to be stiff, and the cat opened wide the two eyes that looked like green lamps, but he closed them again so quickly that Pinocchio did not notice.

"Well now," said the fox, "what will you do with this money?"

"First of all," answered the puppet, "I want to buy my father a beautiful new coat, one that is all silver and gold and has shiny buttons. Then I shall buy a reader for myself."

"For yourself?"

"Certainly. I want to go to school and study hard."

"Look at me," said the fox. "Too much study has cost me the use of a leg."

"Look at me," said the cat. "Too much study has cost me the use of both eyes."

Meanwhile a blackbird that was sitting in a hedge near by sung a single note and said,

"Pinocchio, don't pay attention to the advice of bad companions. If you do, I am sorry for you!"

The poor blackbird might as well have saved its breath. The cat sprang across to it in one jump and, before it could give a squeak, ate it up in one mouthful.

When he had finished and cleaned his mouth, he closed his eyes again and became blind as before.

"Poor blackbird," Pinocchio said to the cat. "Why did you treat him so badly?"

"I did it to teach him a lesson. Next time he will not butt into the conversations of other people."

They had not gone far when the fox stopped suddenly and said to the puppet,

"Do you want to multiply your gold coins?"

"What do you mean?"

"Do you want to change your five miserable coins into a hundred, or a thousand, or two thousand?"

"My word I do! How can it be done?"

"It can be done easily. Instead of returning home, you should come with us."

"And where will you take me?"

"To the country of the Barbagianni."*

"Pinocchio thought for a few minutes, and then said with determination,

"No, I don't want to come. I am near home now, and I want to meet my father who is waiting for me there. Who knows how much the poor old man may have cried for me yesterday when I did not come back. I admit that I have been a bad son, and the Talking Cricket was right when he said, 'Disobedient children cannot have the good things in this life.' I have proved it, because I have already had a number of bad experiences. Yesterday in Mangiafoco's house I was in great danger. Brr! It makes my hair stand on end to think of it!"

"Then you want to go home? Well, go then, and so much the worse for you!"

*Barbagianni means Simpletons in Italian. It is pronounced "Bar-ba-jan-nee."

40

"So much the worse for you!" repeated the cat.

"Think hard, Pinocchio, because you may be passing up a fortune."

"Your five coins will become two thousand between today and tomorrow."

"But how is it possible for them to increase so much?" asked Pinocchio, his mouth open in amazement.

"I'll explain to you straight away," said the fox. "It so happens that in the country of the Barbagianni there is a special field, called by everyone 'The Field of Miracles.' In this field you make a small hole into which you put one of your gold coins. Then you fill in the hole with a little earth, water it with two buckets of water from the fountain, throw a pinch of salt on it, and go home peacefully to your bed. Then, during the night, the coin sprouts and grows. Next morning, you get up and go to the field. And what do you find there? You find a beautiful tree loaded with gold coins, as many as there are grains in a head of ripe corn in the summer."

Pinocchio was still more amazed. "And if I bury my five coins in that field, how many coins will I find there next morning?"

"That is a simple sum," replied the fox. "For every coin that you bury, there will be a bunch of five hundred coins. Multiply five hundred by five, and the next morning you will have in your pocket two thousand five hundred coins, all new and shiny."

"How wonderful!" shouted Pinocchio, dancing with joy. "As soon as I've gathered those coins I'll take two thousand for myself and give five hundred to you two."

"A gift for us!" said the fox. "Please don't speak about it! We would not think of taking anything for ourselves. We work only to make others rich."

"To make others rich," repeated the cat.

"What fine people they are," Pinocchio thought to himself. He completely forgot his father, the new coat, the reader, and all his good resolutions. He said to the fox and the cat, "Let us go. I am coming with you."

CHAPTER 13

What happened at the Inn of the Red Lobster.

They walked for miles and miles, and towards evening they arrived almost dead with tiredness at the Inn of the Red Lobster.

"Let us stop here," said the fox. "We can have something to eat and rest for a few hours. At midnight we shall set out again, and then we'll reach the Field of Miracles by dawn tomorrow."

They went into the inn and sat down at a table, but no one seemed to have a good appetite. The poor cat, who complained of a very sick stomach, could eat only thirty-three fillets of mullet with tomato sauce and four serves of tripe in cheese sauce; and because the tripe was not well enough seasoned, he had to ask three times for butter and grated cheese.

The fox also would have been glad just to nibble at something small, but since the doctor had ordered large meals, he was forced to satisfy himself with merely a large, tender hare served with chicken and fresh mushrooms. After the hare he managed to eat a stew of partridge, pheasant, rabbit, beef, and bird of paradise eggs, but nothing else. He said that the sight of food made him feel so ill that he could not touch another mouthful.

Pinocchio ate least of all. He asked for a piece of walnut and a little bread, and he left everything on the

43

plate. The poor boy's thoughts were fixed so firmly on the Field of Miracles and the gold coins, that he could not eat.

After the meal the fox said to the innkeeper,

"Give us two good rooms, one for Master Pinocchio and the other for my companion and me. We shall take a nap before starting out again. Please be sure to wake us at midnight as we want to continue our journey."

"Yes, sir," answered the innkeeper, and he winked at the fox and the cat as if to say, "I see what you're up to."

Pinocchio was hardly in bed before he fell asleep and began to dream. He seemed to be in the middle of a field, and this field was full of trees with heavily-laden branches, and the branches were weighed down with clusters of gold coins, and these gold coins were swaying in the breeze, so that they made a tinkling sound which almost sounded like "Anyone who wants to can come and take me." But when Pinocchio went up close to them, and reached out his hand to take a handful of all that beautiful money and put it in his pocket, he was woken suddenly by three violent blows on the door of the room.

It was the innkeeper who had come to tell him that it was midnight.

"Are my companions ready?" the puppet asked.

"More than ready! They left two hours ago."

"Why were they in such a hurry?"

"Because the cat received a message that his oldest kitten was sick and in danger of dying."

"And have they paid for the meal?"

"Would you expect them to? They are very refined people, and thought they might insult your lordship."

"What a pity! Such an insult would have given me much pleasure," said Pinocchio, scratching his head. Then he asked,

"And where did my good friends say they will wait for me?"

"At the Field of Miracles, tomorrow at daybreak."

Pinocchio paid one gold coin for the meals, and left the inn.

Outside he had to feel his way along because the night was pitch dark. Not even the stirring of a leaf disturbed the silence. A few night birds, crossing the road from one hedge to the other, brushed their wings on Pinocchio's nose. He jumped backwards with fright and shouted, "Who's there?" The echo from the surrounding hills repeated "Who's there? Who's there? Who's there?"

While he was walking along he noticed on a tree trunk a tiny little animal which shone with a dull, white light, like a candle inside white glass.

"Who are you?" asked Pinocchio.

"I am the ghost of the Talking Cricket," answered the tiny animal, in a very faint little voice which seemed to come from another world.

"What do you want with me?" asked the puppet.

"I want to give you some advice. Turn back and take home to your poor father the four coins that are still left. He is sad and in tears because he has not seen you again."

"Tomorrow my father will be a great lord because these four coins will become two thousand."

"My boy, do not trust those who promise to make you rich between morning and night. As a rule they are either madmen or cheats. Take my advice; listen to me, and turn back."

"But I want to go on."

"The hour is late."

"I want to go on."

"The night is dark."

"I want to go on."

"The road is dangerous."

"I want to go on."

"Remember that boys who always want to have their own way will sooner or later repent it."

"The same old story. Good night, Mr Cricket."

"Good night, Pinocchio, and may heaven save you from the dampness of the night and the highwaymen."

The Talking Cricket then disappeared at once, like the flame of a candle when it is blown out, and the road was even darker than before.

CHAPTER 14

Because he would not take notice of the good advice of the Talking Cricket, Pinocchio encounters the highwaymen.

"How hard life is for us poor boys!" Pinocchio thought to himself as he went on his way. "We are always being scolded, warned, advised. Everyone puts himself in the place of our father or our schoolmaster. Everyone. Even the Talking Cricket. What a nerve! Because I don't want to take notice of that wearisome cricket, he tells me all sorts of terrible things will happen to me! Highwaymen indeed! I don't believe in them, and I never have. They're invented by fathers for the sake of scaring children who want to go out in the night. And what if I should meet them here on the road? Would I be frightened? Not on your life! I'd go straight up to them and say, 'What do you highwaymen want with me? And no silly business. Now go about your own affairs, and be quick about it.' When those poor highwaymen heard me speak like that, they'd go like the wind. I can almost see them. And if by chance they're too ignorant to want to escape, then I shall escape, and so the affair will finish . . .'"

But Pinocchio was not able to finish his little story because at that moment he seemed to hear behind him a slight rustling of the leaves. He turned and saw in the dark the outlines of two black figures all wrapped up in coal sacks. They were running quietly behind him on the tips of their toes, like two phantoms.

47

"Here they are really!" he said to himself, and not knowing where to hide his four coins, he slipped them into his mouth and under his tongue.

Then he tried to escape, but he could not take a step before he felt himself grabbed by the arms and heard two deep, horrible voices which said, "Your money or your life!"

Pinocchio did not want to speak because of the money in his mouth, so he made many bows and gave all sorts of signs to show the hooded pair that he was only a poor little puppet who did not have even one cent in his pocket. All he could see of the highwaymen was their eyes through holes in the sacks.

"Enough of that nonsense! Out with the money!" said the two robbers menacingly.

The puppet made signs with his head and hands as if to say, "I have none."

"Let's have the money or you're dead!" said the taller highwayman.

"Dead!" repeated the other.

"And after we've murdered you, we'll murder your father too."

"Your father too!"

"No, no, no! Not my poor father!" cried Pinocchio desperately, and the cry made the coins knock together noisily in his mouth.

"Ah, scoundrel! So you've hidden the coins under your tongue. Spit them out, and be quick about it!"

But Pinocchio did not move.

"Deaf, are you? We'll see in a moment whether you'll spit them out!"

Then one of them seized the puppet by the point of his nose and the other by his chin, and they began to pull roughly, one in one direction and one in the other, to force him to open his mouth. But they could not do it. The puppet's mouth seemed to be firmly nailed and bolted.

Next the shorter of the two highwaymen took out a

48

knife and tried to drive it between his lips like a lever or chisel. Pinocchio acted as quick as lightning. He seized the hand between his teeth, bit a piece off cleanly, and spat it out. You can imagine his surprise when he noticed that what he spat on the ground was not a hand but a cat's paw.

This first victory gave him courage. He wrenched free from the grip of the highwaymen, jumped the hedge on the side of the road, and ran off across the countryside. The highwaymen chased after him like two dogs after a hare. The one who had lost a paw ran on one front leg only, but it did not slow him down.

After running for about ten miles, Pinocchio could not go any further. Just when he was sure he would be caught, he came to a huge pine tree. He clambered quickly up the trunk to a position high up among the top boughs. The highwaymen tried to climb up after him, but when they were halfway they slipped and fell to the ground, taking the skin off their hands and feet.

However they did not give up. Instead they collected a bundle of dry wood, placed it around the bottom of the tree, and set fire to it. In less than a minute the pine tree began to blaze and shoot out tongues of flame like a candle blown in the wind. Pinocchio saw the flames climbing closer to him all the time. He did not want to finish up like a roast pigeon, so he made a big jump from the top of the tree and ran away once more across the fields and vineyards. The highwaymen kept running behind him, never seeming to tire.

While Pinocchio ran the morning light began to show in the sky. All of a sudden he found his way barred by a very deep and broad ditch which was full of smelly, muddy water. What should he do? "One, two, three!..." cried the puppet and, launching himself in full flight, he jumped to the other side. The highwaymen also jumped, but they had not judged so well, and ker-plonk!... they fell right in the middle of the ditch.

When Pinocchio heard the thud and the splashes, he laughed and cried out, "Have a nice swim, you highwaymen."

He believed they were well and truly drowned when, looking back, he found them running along behind him, still wrapped up in their sacks and dripping water like two buckets full of holes.

CHAPTER 15

The highwaymen keep on chasing Pinocchio, and when they catch him they hang him to the bough of the Giant Oak tree.

By this time the puppet was exhausted. He was on the point of throwing himself on the ground and giving up when he saw among the trees of the forest a little house, white as snow, shining brightly in the distance.

"If I can find the breath to reach that house, perhaps I shall be saved," he said to himself. And without waiting a moment he started running through the woods again at full speed. The highwaymen kept on behind him.

After a desperate chase of almost two hours he finally arrived, completely breathless, at the door of the little house, and knocked.

No one came.

He knocked again more violently, because he could hear the noise of footsteps behind him and the heavy, panting breath of his enemies. Still no noise came from the house.

As the knocking had no effect, he kicked and thumped desperately at the door. Then a beautiful young girl appeared at the window. She had raven-coloured hair and her face was as white as a wax image; her eyes were closed and her hands were crossed on her chest. Without moving her lips at all she spoke in a faint voice that seemed to come from another world.

"There is no one in this house. They are all dead."

"Then won't you let me in?" shouted Pinocchio, weeping and pleading.

"I too am dead."

"Dead? Then what are you doing there at the window?"

"I am waiting for the coffin that is coming to take me away."

Then the girl disappeared and the window closed itself without making a noise.

"Oh dear, beautiful girl, please let me in! Have pity on a poor boy chased by two highway . . . ."

But he could not finish the word. He was grabbed by the neck and the same two rough voices rumbled at him, "You won't escape again!"

The poor little puppet, feeling that death was near, trembled so violently that the joints of his wooden legs rattled and so did the four coins hidden under his tongue.

"Well?" said the highwaymen. "Will you open your mouth now? Yes or no? Ah! No answer! Don't worry. This time we'll open it for you!"

They each drew out a very long knife, sharp as a razor, and stabbed him twice in the middle of the back.

But, by good luck, the puppet was made of very hard wood, and this caused the blades of the knives to break into a thousand pieces. The highwaymen were left with the handles in their hands.

"I know," said the taller one. "We must hang him. Let's hang him!"

"Let's hang him!" repeated the other.

They bound his hands behind him, passed a noose with a slip knot over his head, and hung him from the bough of a very large tree called the Giant Oak.

They then sat down on the grass below and waited for the puppet to breathe his last breath. But after three hours the puppet still had his eyes open, his mouth shut, and was as frisky as ever.

At length the highwaymen became tired of waiting,

52

and they said roughly to Pinocchio, "Goodbye for the present. When we return tomorrow, we hope that you will do us the courtesy of being well and truly dead, with your mouth wide open."

And they went away.

Before long a strong north wind blew up. It whistled and roared fiercely, knocking about poor little Pinocchio as he hung there, and making him swing back and forth violently like the clapper of a bell on a church day. The swinging sent sharp pains through him, and the slip knot slowly tightened around his neck, stopping his breath.

Little by little his eyes dimmed over and he felt that he was going to die. Yet he never gave up hope that at some moment a kind person would turn up and save him. But when, after a long time, no one appeared, his thoughts turned to his poor father. He muttered faintly, on the point of death, "Oh my dear daddy, if only you were here!"

He did not have the breath left to say another word. He closed his eyes, opened his mouth, stretched his legs, gave a big shake, and hung still and stiff.

CHAPTER 16

The beautiful girl with the raven-coloured hair has the puppet taken down from the tree. She puts him to bed and calls three doctors to find out whether he is dead or alive.

Just at that moment when poor Pinocchio, hanging from a bough of the Giant Oak, seemed more dead than alive, the beautiful girl with the raven-coloured hair appeared again at the window. She was moved to pity by the sad sight of Pinocchio, hanging by the neck, dancing wildly in the gusts of the north wind. She clapped her hands three times.

At this signal there was a loud noise of wings beating furiously, and a large falcon came and perched on the window sill.

"What is your wish, my gentle Fairy?" said the falcon, lowering his beak as a mark of respect (because you must now be told that the girl with the raven-coloured hair was really a good fairy who, for more than a thousand years, had lived in the neighbourhood of that wood).

"Do you see that puppet hanging by a rope to the bough of the Giant Oak?"

"I see him."

"Fly down there at once. Use your very strong beak to break the knot that is holding him in the air, and take him and lay him very gently on the grass at the foot of the Giant Oak."

The falcon flew away, and after two minutes he returned and said, "What you ordered has been done."

"And how did you find him? Alive or dead?"

"He seemed dead by his appearance, but he may not yet be quite dead because, after I had loosened the knot that was choking him, he gave a sigh and whispered, 'Now I feel better'."

The Fairy clapped her hands twice, and a magnificent poodle appeared, walking upright on its hind legs, just like a man. The poodle was dressed in the sort of outfit a coachman might wear for a special occasion. He wore on his head a little three-pointed cap trimmed with gold braid, and a white wig with curls that hung to his shoulders. His jacket was a rich brown colour with bright silver buttons and two large pockets for holding the bones that his mistress gave him at meal time. His short pants were of crimson velvet, his stockings were silk, his little shoes were cut away at the top, and hanging behind him there was a type of lined umbrella case, made of blue satin, to hold his tail if it should begin to rain.

"A special task for you, my good Medoro!" the Fairy said to the poodle. "Go at once and prepare the best coach in my stable. Then take the road through the woods. When you reach the Great Oak you will find on the grass a poor little puppet who is almost dead. Pick him up carefully, lay him gently on the cushions in the coach, and bring him to me. Is that clear?"

The poodle showed that he had understood by wagging his blue satin tail cover three or four times, and departed at high speed.

Within a few minutes a beautiful little coach emerged from the stable. It was pale blue and was padded all over with canary feathers. The inside was lined with whipped cream and light custard. The little coach was drawn by a hundred pairs of small white mice and the poodle, seated on the box, shook his whip from right to left, as a driver does when he is afraid of being late.

Not a quarter of an hour had passed before the coach returned. The Fairy was standing on the doorstep

waiting. She took the puppet in her arms and carried him to a small room with mother-of-pearl walls. She then sent immediately for the three best doctors in the district.

The doctors arrived one after the other: a crow, an owl, and a Talking Cricket.

The Fairy turned to the three doctors who had gathered around Pinocchio's bed and said, "I should like to know from you three gentlemen if this unfortunate puppet is alive or dead."

The crow pushed forward in front of the others. He felt Pinocchio's pulse; then he touched his nose; then his little toe. And when he had made all these tests carefully he spoke these words solemnly: "In my opinion the puppet is quite dead; but if by some chance he is not dead, then it will be a sure indication that he is still alive!"

"It is my unpleasant duty," said the owl, "to have to contradict my illustrious friend and colleague, the crow. It is my opinion that the puppet is still alive; but if by some chance he is not alive, then it is a sign that he is certainly dead."

"Have you nothing to say?" the Fairy asked the Talking Cricket.

"I say that it is wiser for a doctor when he does not know what to say, to say nothing at all. However, that puppet's face is not new to me. I met him a short time ago!"

Until then Pinocchio had been as motionless as a real piece of wood, but he suddenly gave a great shiver which made the whole bed shake.

"This puppet here," continued the Talking Cricket, "is a dyed-in-the-wool villain. . . ."

Pinocchio opened his eyes and shut them again.

"He's a lazy, good-for-nothing vagabond. . . ."

Pinocchio hid his face under the sheet.

"This puppet is a disobedient son who will make his poor father die of a broken heart!"

At this point there was heard in the room a suffocated noise of crying and sobbing. You can imagine everyone's surprise when, upon lifting the sheet a little, they found that it was Pinocchio who was crying and sobbing.

"When a dead person cries, it is a sign that he is on the way to recovery," said the crow solemnly.

"It pains me to contradict my illustrious friend and colleague," added the owl, "but, in my opinion, when a dead person cries it is a sign that he does not want to die."

CHAPTER 17

Pinocchio eats the lump of sugar, but will not take his medicine. However when he sees the grave-diggers who come to take him away, he changes his mind. Then he tells a lie, and as punishment his nose grows.

When the three doctors had left the room, the Fairy came close to Pinocchio's bed. She felt his forehead and could tell that he had a very high fever. She dropped a little white powder into half a glass of water, handed it to the puppet, and said in a gentle voice,

"Drink this, and you will soon be better."

Pinocchio looked at the glass, made a wry face, and asked in a whimpering voice,

"Is it sweet or bitter?"

"It's bitter, but it will cure you."

"If it's bitter, I don't want it."

"Do as I say and drink it."

"I don't like bitter things."

"Drink it, and then I will give you a lump of sugar to take the taste away."

"Where's the lump of sugar?"

"Here it is," said the Fairy, holding up a golden sugar basin.

"First I want the lump of sugar, and then I'll drink that bitter stuff."

"You promise me?"

"Yes."

The Fairy gave him the lump, and Pinocchio crunched it up and swallowed it in a moment. He licked his lips and said,

"What a good thing if sugar were a medicine! I'd take medicine every day."

"Now keep your promise and drink this little glass of water that will make you better."

Pinocchio took the glass unwillingly and put it up to his nose; then he put it near his lips; then he put it to his nose again. Finally he said,

"It's too bitter! Too bitter! I cannot drink it."

"How can you say that, if you haven't even tried?"

"I can tell. I've tasted the smell. First I want another lump of sugar. Then I'll drink it."

So the Fairy, with all the patience of a good mother, put another lump of sugar in his mouth, and again offered the glass to him.

"No, I still can't drink it," said the puppet, pulling all sorts of faces.

"Why?"

"That sheet on my feet is hurting me."

The Fairy lifted the sheet away from him.

"It's hopeless! I cannot possibly drink it."

"What else is troubling you?"

"The door there, the way it's half open."

The Fairy went and closed the door.

"I can't!" cried Pinocchio with a big sob. "I can't drink that bitter stuff. No, no, no!"

"My boy, I beg you. . . ."

"I don't care. . . ."

"Your illness is serious. . . ."

"I don't care. . . ."

"You cannot live more than a couple of hours with that fever. . . ."

"I don't care. . . ."

"Aren't you afraid of dying?"

"Not at all! . . . I'd rather die than drink that nasty medicine."

Just then the door of the room sprung open and in walked four rabbits, all as black as ink. They carried a small coffin on their shoulders.

"What do you want with me?" cried Pinocchio as he tried to sit up. He was now very frightened.

"We have come to take you away," answered the biggest rabbit.

"Take me away? But I am not yet dead!"

"Not yet, but you have only a few minutes left because you refused to take the medicine which would have cured the fever."

"Oh my dear Fairy, my good Fairy," the puppet called out, "give me the glass quickly. Hurry, please, I don't want to die! I don't want to die!"

He took the glass in both hands and swallowed it in a mouthful.

"Bad luck!" said the rabbits. "This time we've made the journey in vain."

They put the little coffin back on their shoulders and left the room, grumbling and muttering among themselves.

Within a few minutes Pinocchio jumped down from the bed, completely cured. (I must tell you that wooden puppets have the natural gift of seldom falling ill and of getting better very quickly.)

When the Fairy saw him running and jumping around the room, as gay and lively as a lamb in springtime, she said,

"My medicine has certainly done you good, I see."

"It's done more than that; it has brought me back to life."

"Then why did you make so much fuss about taking it?"

"It's just that we boys are all the same. We're more afraid of medicine than of the illness."

"Shame on you! Boys ought to know that good medicine taken in time can save them from serious illness, and perhaps from death. . . ."

"Another time I will not make such a fuss. I'll think of those black rabbits with the coffin on their shoulders. Then I'll take the glass at once, and down it will go!"

"Well then, come here to me and tell me how you came to fall into the hands of the highwaymen."

"It all started when the puppeteer, Mangiafoco, gave me some gold coins and said to me, 'Take these, and give them to your father,' but instead of doing that I met on the road a fox and a cat, two very nice animals, who said to me, 'Do you want those few coins to become one or two thousand? Come with us, and we'll take you to the Field of Miracles.' I said, 'Let us go,' and they said, 'We'll stop here at the Inn of the Red Lobster, and after midnight we'll set out again.' And when I woke up they were no longer there because they had left. Then I began to walk through the night, which was as black as could be, and on the way I came upon two highwaymen wearing black sacks, who said to me, 'Hand over your money,' and I said, 'I haven't any,' because I had hidden those four gold coins in my mouth, and one of the highwaymen tried to put his hand in my mouth, and I bit it clean off and spat it out, but instead of a hand I spat out the paw of a cat. The highwaymen chased me and I ran and ran, until they caught me and hung me by the neck from a tree in this wood, and said to me, 'We'll come back tomorrow, and then you'll be dead with your mouth open, and we'll take the gold coins that you've hidden under your tongue.'"

"And where are the four coins now?" asked the Fairy.

"I lost them!" answered Pinocchio, but he told a lie, because he had them in his pocket.

He had hardly uttered the lie before his nose, which was long already, grew another two inches.

"And where did you lose them?"

"In the woods quite near here."

At this second lie, his nose grew longer.

"If that is so," said the Fairy, "we'll search and find them, because everything that is lost in these woods is found."

"Wait a minute! I've just remembered," replied the

puppet, becoming confused, "I didn't lose the coins. I swallowed them by mistake when I took your medicine."

At this third lie, his nose grew so long in such a short time that poor Pinocchio could no longer move. If he turned one way he knocked his nose on the bed or the window, and if another, he knocked it against the walls or the door; if he lifted his head a little, he ran the risk of poking it in the eye of the Fairy.

The Fairy looked at him and laughed.

"Why are you laughing?" asked the puppet, all flustered and upset because his nose grew while he looked at it.

"I am laughing at the lies that you've told."

"How do you know that I've told lies?"

"Lies are easily recognized, my boy, because there are two kinds. There are lies that have short legs, and lies that have long noses. Yours are obviously of the kind that have a long nose."

Pinocchio was so ashamed that he did not know where to hide himself, and he tried to run from the room. But he did not succeed. His nose had grown so much that it would not fit through the door.

CHAPTER 18

*Pinocchio meets the fox and
the cat again and goes with
them to sow his four coins in
the Field of Miracles.*

The Fairy let the puppet cry and scream for a good half
an hour, and the reason for all the noise was that
Pinocchio's nose would no longer pass through the
door of the room. Then she gave him a severe lecture
in the hope of correcting that very ugly habit of telling
lies, the worst habit that a boy can have. When at last
she saw him quite changed, his eyes almost standing
out of his head with shame and confusion, she took
pity on him. She clapped her hands, and on this signal
thousands of large woodpeckers flew in through the
window. They sat all along Pinocchio's nose and began
pecking away at such a pace that in a few minutes the
long, thick nose was reduced to its natural size.

"How good you are, my dear Fairy," said the puppet,
drying his eyes. "I love you very much."

"I love you too, Pinocchio," replied the Fairy, "and
if you want to, you can stay with me and be my little
brother and I will be your little sister."

"I will stay gladly, but what about my poor father?"

"I have thought of everything. Your father has
already been told, and he will be here before night."

"Really?" cried Pinocchio, jumping with happiness.
"May I please go to meet him? I long to kiss that dear
old man who has suffered so much for me."

"You may go, but be careful not to get lost. Take the

path through the woods and you will be certain to meet him."

Pinocchio left, and was soon running along through the woods like a young deer. He had almost reached the Great Oak when he stopped because he thought that he heard voices among the trees. Suddenly he saw before him on the road . . . can you guess who? . . . the fox and the cat, the two companions on his earlier journey, with whom he had dined at the Inn of the Red Lobster.

"Here is our dear friend, Pinocchio," cried the fox, embracing him and kissing him. "How did you ever come to be here?"

"How did you ever come to be here?" repeated the cat.

"It's a long story," said the puppet, "but I'll try to tell you everything. First of all, the other night when you left me alone in the Inn I met two highwaymen on the road. . . ."

"Highwaymen! Oh, my poor friend! What did they want?"

"They wanted to steal my gold coins."

"How terrible!" said the fox.

"How very terrible!" said the cat.

"But I began to run away," the puppet continued, "and they ran after me, until they caught me and hung me on a branch of that oak tree." And Pinocchio pointed to the Great Oak, which was not more than two yards away.

"Can one think of anything worse?" said the fox. "In what sort of a world are we condemned to live? Where shall gentlemen like us find a safe place?"

While they were talking in this way Pinocchio noticed that the cat was lame on one of his front legs because his paw was missing. "What have you done to your paw?" he asked.

The cat tried to say something but became confused. Then the fox said quickly, "My friend is too modest and that is why he doesn't answer. Let me answer for him. Not more than an hour ago we met on the road an old wolf who was almost dying of hunger. He begged us to give him something. We did not have even the backbone of a fish with us, so what do you think my friend here did, my friend with such a good, brave heart? He bit off his own front paw and threw it to that poor beast so that he could have something to eat." And as he said this, the fox dried away a tear.

Pinocchio was very moved, and came up to the cat and whispered in his ear, "If all cats were the same as you, wouldn't the birds be lucky?"

"And what are you doing in this place?" the fox asked the puppet.

"I am waiting for my father who should arrive at any moment now."

"And what about your gold coins?"

"I have them in my pocket, except for the one that I used to pay for the meal at the Inn of the Red Lobster."

"Just to think that instead of those four coins you could have by tomorrow a thousand, or maybe two thousand! Why don't you take my advice? Why don't you come with us and sow them in the Field of Miracles?"

"It is impossible today. I shall go with you another day."

"Another day will be too late," said the fox.

"Why?"

"Because that field has been bought by an important man, and from tomorrow it will not be possible for anyone to go in there to sow their money."

"How far from here is the Field of Miracles?"

"Hardly two miles. Do you want to come with us? Within half an hour you will be there. You can sow the four coins immediately, and after a few minutes you will gather two thousand. By this evening you will return here with your pockets full. Why don't you come with us?"

Pinocchio hesitated a little before he answered,

because he remembered the good Fairy, old Geppetto, and the warnings of the Talking Cricket. But then he finished by doing what all little boys do who lack a sense of justice and have no feeling in their heart. He finished, that is to say, with shrugging his shoulders and saying to the fox and the cat, "Let us go then. I will come with you." And they set off.

After having walked for half a day they arrived at a city which had the name *Catch-a-Fool*. As soon as they entered Pinocchio saw that the streets were full of the strangest sights. There were mangy dogs with mouths hanging open from hunger, sheep without fleeces who trembled in the cold, hens without combs or wattles who begged for a grain of wheat, large butterflies who could not fly because they had sold their beautiful wings, peacocks with their tail feathers all gone who were ashamed to be seen, and pheasants who were wandering about quietly, regretting the loss of their beautiful wings of gold and silver.

From time to time richly decorated carriages passed through this crowd of poor, sad beasts, and in them were foxes, thieving magpies, or other birds of prey.

"Where is the Field of Miracles?" Pinocchio asked.

"Not far from here," said the fox.

They crossed the city and came out the gate in the wall on the other side, and then stopped in a lonely field which looked just like any other field.

"Here we are," the fox said to the puppet. "Now bend down to the ground, scrape out a little hole with your hands, and put in your gold coins."

Pinocchio did as he was asked. He dug out a hole, put in the four coins, and covered them with a little earth.

"Now," said the fox, "go to that pond over there, take a bucketful of water, and sprinkle the ground where you have sown."

Pinocchio went to the pond and, because he did not have a bucket with him, picked up an old shoe that was lying there, filled it with water, and sprinkled the earth over the hole. Then he asked, "Is there anything else to do?"

"Nothing at all," answered the fox. "Now we shall go away. When you return here in about twenty minutes you will find that a tree has shot up in the soil and that its boughs are loaded with money."

The poor puppet, beside himself with happiness, thanked the fox and the cat a thousand times and promised them a fine gift.

"We do not want anything at all," answered those two rogues. "For us it is enough to have been able to show you the way to get rich without hard work. That alone makes us as happy as the day is long."

Then they said goodbye to Pinnochio, wished him a good harvest, and went off about their own affairs.

CHAPTER 19

Pinocchio is robbed of his gold coins and as punishment he is sent to prison for four months.

The puppet returned to the city and began to count the minutes one by one. When it seemed to him that the time had passed he immediately set off on the road that led back to the Field of Miracles.

As he walked along quickly his excitement made his heart beat fast, and it made a sharp noise, tick-tock, tick-tock, tick-tock, like a large clock. All the time he was thinking to himself, "And if instead of a thousand coins, I find two thousand on the boughs of the tree, won't that be wonderful? And what if, instead of two thousand, I find five thousand? And if instead of five thousand, I find one hundred thousand? Oh, what a great lord I shall become then. I should like to have a fine mansion, thousands of wooden horses with stables to amuse myself with, a pantry full of cordials and soft drinks, a library full of crystallized fruit, tarts, fruit cakes, marshmallow, and cream-puffs."

Dreaming in this way, he soon arrived near the field and stopped to look, just in case he could make out some trees with branches full of money, but he saw nothing. He took another hundred paces forward, and still saw nothing. He entered the field and went right up to the little hole where he had buried his coins, but the ground was bare. Then he became thoughtful and, forgetting what he had been taught about good manners and correct behaviour, he took his hand out of his pocket and scratched his head thoughtfully.

Meanwhile he heard a laughing noise near by, and turning around he saw above him in a tree a large parrot who was cleaning the few feathers that he still had left.

"Why are you laughing?" Pinocchio asked in an angry voice.

"Because in cleaning my feathers I tickled myself under the wing," answered the parrot.

The puppet did not reply. He went to the pond and filled the same old shoe with water and used it again to sprinkle the ground where he had buried his gold coins.

Just then there was more laughter, this time cheekier than before, and it sounded very loud in the silence.

Pinocchio became angry. He called out, "Will you please tell me what you are laughing at, you silly parrot."

"I am laughing at the thought of those simple people who believe every stupid thing they are told and so let themselves be tricked by those who are more cunning than they are."

"You speak of me perhaps?"

"Yes, I am speaking about you, my poor Pinocchio, because you were so silly as to believe that coins may be sown and harvested in the fields as one sows beans and pumpkin. I too believed that once, and now I am suffering for it. At last (too late alas!) I have learnt by hard experience, and will now tell you, that to put together a little money honestly you must work with your own hands or with your own brain."

"I don't understand you," said the puppet who was already beginning to tremble with fear.

"What a pity! I shall explain myself more clearly. While you were in the city the fox and the cat returned to this field, took the gold coins buried here, and then fled away like the wind. And now it will take a clever fellow to catch them!"

Pinocchio stood with his mouth wide open, not wanting to believe the parrot. He began to dig in the ground with his hands and fingernails and to scoop out the earth where he had watered. He dug and dug and dug and made such a large hole that a haystack could have stood there upright, but the money was not to be found.

Then, in despair, he returned to the city at a run and went at once to the Courthouse to denounce to the judge the thieves who had robbed him.

The magistrate was an ape of the gorilla variety, a very old gorilla who was much respected for his age and serious manner, for his white beard, and especially for his spectacles of gold without glass in them, which he was obliged to wear because of an inflammation of the eyes that had troubled him for several years.

In the presence of the magistrate Pinocchio told in detail the story of the nasty fraud of which he had been a victim. He gave the full names and descriptions of the thieves, and finished by asking for justice.

The magistrate listened to him with great kindness. He took the most lively interest in the story. He appeared very sorry for Pinocchio. And when the puppet had finished and had nothing more to say, the magistrate stretched out his hand and rang the bell.

At this sound there appeared at once two blood-hounds dressed in the clothes of policemen.

The magistrate nodded towards Pinocchio and said to the policemen, "This poor fellow has been robbed of four gold coins. Take him and put him in prison at once." The puppet was quite overcome when he heard this sentence. He just stood there in amazement trying to think of something to say in protest. But the policemen, to avoid a useless waste of time, covered his mouth and led him away to prison.

And there he had to remain for four months—four very long months indeed. And he would have had to stay there even longer but for a lucky chance.

At this point I must tell my readers that the young emperor who reigned in the city of Catch-a-fool had just won a great victory against his enemies and had ordered a public holiday, with a fireworks display and horse and bicycle races. Also, to mark the great happiness of the occasion, he gave orders that the prisons would be opened and that all the prisoners would be set free.

Pinocchio said to his guard, "If the others in the prison are to be set free, I want to get out also."

"Oh no, not you," answered the guard. "You are not like the others."

"I beg to differ," replied Pinocchio. "I am indeed a thief like the others."

"In that case you may go free," said the guard. He lifted his hat respectfully, saluted, opened the gate of the prison, and let Pinocchio escape.

CHAPTER 20

Once he is freed from prison Pinocchio sets out to return to the Fairy's house but along the way he comes upon a terrible snake and is then caught in a trap.

You can imagine the happiness of Pinocchio when he realized that he was free. Without stopping to do anything, he set out at once towards the city and took again the road that would lead him back to the Fairy's house.

Because of the wet weather the road had become very boggy, and anyone going on it was likely to sink up to their knees in the mud. But the puppet did not take any notice because he was so anxious to see his father and his dear little sister with the raven-coloured hair. He ran along with leaps and bounds like a greyhound, splashing mud from the top of his head to the tips of his toes. He said to himself, "How many misfortunes have happened to me! And I deserved them all because I have been a nasty, selfish puppet. I always wanted to do the things that pleased me without paying attention to those who know better and who have a thousand times more sense than I have! But from this moment I make a resolution to change my way of life and to become a thoughtful and obedient boy. I have had plenty of opportunity to see that boys who are disobedient will always get themselves into trouble and never succeed in anything. And what of my poor father who has been waiting for me? Will I find him at the Fairy's house? It is such a long time since I have seen the poor man that I long to hug him and kiss him a million times. And will the Fairy pardon me for the bad things I have done? Just to think how much goodness and love she has heaped on me. . . . But for her I would not be alive today! How could any boy be more ungrateful and heartless than I am?"

While he was saying this he stopped suddenly with fright and took four paces backwards.

What do you think he had seen?

He had seen an immense snake stretched across the road. It had green skin, fiery eyes, and a pointed tail that sent out smoke like the top of a chimney.

You could not possibly imagine how frightened the puppet was. He drew himself back some hundreds of yards and sat down on a little hill of stones to wait for the snake to go about his own business so that the road would be free.

He waited one hour . . . two . . . three. But the snake was still there, and even from a distance he seemed to be glowing from his eyes and the plume of smoke kept rising from the point of his tail.

Then Pinocchio screwed up his courage and approached to within a few steps of the snake. He said in a soft, coaxing voice, "Excuse me, Mr Snake, but would you be kind enough to draw a little to one side so that I may pass?"

He might as well have talked to a wall; there was no movement at all.

Then Pinocchio said again in the same soft voice, "Please, Mr Snake, I am on my way home where my father is waiting for me and it's such a long time since I have seen him. Could you please let me pass by?"

He waited for some kind of answer to his question, but the answer did not come. Instead, the snake, who until then had seemed bright and full of life became quite still and almost stiff. His eyes closed and the tail stopped smoking.

74

"I wonder if he is dead," said Pinocchio, rubbing his hands together happily. Without waiting any longer, he made as if to jump over the snake in order to continue along the road. But he had not even lifted his leg when the snake rose up suddenly like a spring let loose and the puppet, drawing back with fright, tripped over and fell on the ground. He fell so heavily that he was fixed with his head stuck in the muddy road and his legs up in the air. At the sight of the puppet, kicking wildly upside down, the snake was taken by a sudden fit of laughing, and he laughed and laughed and laughed until from the effort of so much laughing he broke a vein in his chest, and this time he was really dead.

Then Pinocchio began to run along the road again in order to reach the Fairy's house before it was dark. But as he went along he began to suffer from terrible pangs of hunger, and when he could stand them no longer he jumped into a field to pick a few small bunches of grapes.

It would have been better for him if he never had! He had hardly managed to get under the vine when—crack! He felt two iron jaws close on his legs and he seemed to see all the stars in the sky. The poor puppet had been caught in a trap placed there by a farmer in order to catch some large weasels who had been raiding all the hen-yards in the district.

CHAPTER 21

Pinocchio is caught by a farmer who forces him to act as a watch-dog over a hen-yard.

Pinocchio cried and screamed at the top of his voice, but he was only wasting his time, because there was no one to hear him.

Meanwhile night came on.

The puppet was in great pain because the jaws of the trap were cutting into his shins, and he was very frightened at being all alone in the dark. He began to feel that he would faint, when all of a sudden he saw a firefly.

"Firefly," he called out, "would you be so good as to free me from this trap?"

"My poor boy," replied the firefly, stopping in pity and looking at him. "How did you ever come to get your legs caught in those iron jaws?"

"I climbed into the field to pick a bunch of these juicy grapes."

"Are they your grapes?"

"No."

"Then who taught you that you could take another person's goods?"

"I was hungry."

"Hunger, my dear boy, is no excuse for stealing."

"You're right! You're right!" cried Pinocchio. "I shall never do it again."

At this point the conversation was interrupted by a

very faint noise of approaching footsteps. It was the owner of the field who was coming on the tips of his toes to see if one of those weasels who were eating his hens in the night had been caught in the jaws of the trap. He took his lantern from beneath his overcoat and was very surprised to discover that instead of a weasel he had caught a boy.

"Well, my little thief!" said the farmer, becoming angry. "So you are the one who has been stealing my chickens."

"Not me! Not me!" cried Pinocchio sobbing. "I came into the field to take only a bunch of grapes."

"Anyone who is capable of stealing grapes is just as capable of stealing hens. What a fine thing! I'll give you a lesson that you won't forget for a long time."

He opened the trap, grabbed the puppet by the scruff of the neck and carried him almost as far as the house as if he were a small lamb.

When they reached the threshing floor he dropped the puppet roughly on the ground and said to him, "It's late now and I'm going to bed. We'll settle our account in the morning, but meanwhile I have a little job for you. My faithful watch-dog died today, so you can take his place."

Without delay he put around Pinocchio's neck a thick collar covered with brass spikes and pulled it tight so that there would be no chance of his passing his head through it. A long iron chain was attached to the collar and fixed onto the wall.

Then the farmer said, "If it should rain tonight you can go and lie down in that wooden kennel. There's always straw in it. It has served as a bed for four years for my poor little dog. And if by any chance the thieves should come, remember to keep your ears open and to bark."

After this last warning the farmer entered his house, closed the door, bolted it and made it fast with a padlock. Poor Pinocchio remained crouching on the threshing floor, feeling more dead than alive. He was cold, hungry and afraid. From time to time he pulled fiercely at the collar which was hurting him and cried sadly, "It serves me right! Yes, it serves me right! I have always been a good-for-nothing and a vagabond. I listened to bad companions and because of that I've always fallen into trouble. If I had been a good boy, as some are, if I had studied and worked, if I had stayed in my poor old father's house, at this moment I wouldn't find myself here in the middle of the fields acting as a watch-dog for this farmer. Oh, if only I could be born again! But now it's too late and I must be patient!"

These words from the bottom of his heart gave him some relief, and he went into the kennel and soon fell asleep.

Pinocchio discovers the thieves and as a reward for being faithful he is set free.

22

He had already been sleeping soundly for two hours when towards midnight he was awakened by a whispering and chattering of strange voices that seemed to come from the threshing floor. He put his nose out of the kennel and saw a group of four little beasts with dark skins that looked like cats. They were not cats, but weasels: small carnivorous animals with a very great appetite, especially for eggs and chickens. One of these weasels broke away from the group and went to the door of the kennel. He said in a low voice, "Good evening, Melampo."

"My name is not Melampo," answered the puppet.

"Then who are you?"

"I am Pinocchio."

"And what are you doing here?"

"I am the watch-dog."

"Then where is Melampo? Where is the old dog who always used to live in this kennel.?"

"He died this morning."

"Dead? Poor beast! He was a good friend. But judging by your face you also seem to be a well-mannered dog."

"I beg your pardon. I am not a dog."

"Oh, what are you?"

"I am a puppet."

"And what are you doing as a watch-dog?"

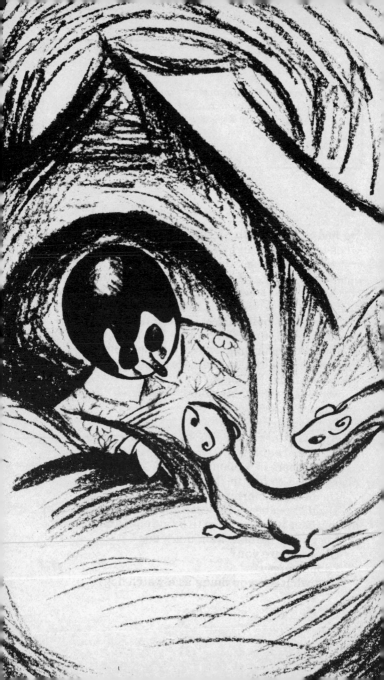

"Alas! It is my punishment."

"Well then, I offer you the same arrangement that we had with poor old Melampo, and I'm sure you will be happy with it."

"And what arrangement was this?"

"We shall see you once a week when we come to visit the hens at night. We'll take eight hens, and of these we'll eat seven and give one to you, on this condition: you must pretend to sleep, and do not take it into your head to bark and wake the farmer."

"Is this what Melampo did?" asked the puppet.

"Yes, he did, and we always got on very well together. You sleep quietly now, and you may be sure that before leaving here we'll leave at your door a hen that has been plucked and is ready to eat. You understand what we mean?"

"Yes, very well!" replied the puppet, and in the dark he nodded his head fiercely as if to say, "We'll see about that!"

When the four weasels believed that they were safe to go about their business, they went one after another to the hen-yard which was just next to the dog kennel. They made an opening by biting furiously with their teeth and claws at the little wooden door that covered the entrance, and then slipped inside. But they had hardly entered when they heard the little door close with a great slam. It was Pinocchio who had closed it, and not content with that, he leant a large rock against it to make quite sure they could not escape.

Then he began to bark very loudly, just like a dog, "Woof, woof, woof, woof."

At the sound of his barking the farmer jumped from his bed, took a gun that was leaning against the window, and called out, "What's the matter now?"

"There are thieves!" replied Pinocchio.

"Where are they?"

"In the hen-yard."

"I'll be down in a moment."

And in less time than it takes to say "amen" the farmer came down and ran into the hen-yard. He quickly caught the four weasels and put them in a sack. Then he said to them in a very pleased voice, "At last you've fallen into my hands! I could punish you, but nothing would be bad enough! Instead of that I'll take you tomorrow to the innkeeper at the village near by. He'll skin you and cook you just like nice little rabbits. It is an honour that you don't deserve, but generous men like me do not like to act meanly!"

Then, coming to Pinocchio, he gave him many friendly pats and said among other things, "How did you come to discover the scheme of these four little thieves? And just to think that Melampo, my faithful Melampo, was never aware of anything!"

The puppet could have told what he knew. He could have described the shameful arrangement between the dog and the weasels. But he remembered that the dog was dead and he thought to himself immediately, "What good does it do to blame the dead? The dead are dead, and the best thing that one can do is to leave them in peace."

The farmer asked him, "Were you awake or asleep when the weasels turned up?"

"I was asleep," replied the puppet, "but the weasels woke me with their chattering, and one of them finally came to the door of the kennel and said to me, 'If you promise not to bark and wake up the master we will give you a chicken that is plucked and ready to eat.' What do you think of that? Fancy having the cheek to suggest such a thing to me! I'm only a puppet and no better than most people, but I'm not capable of joining a gang and stealing the property of honest people!"

"Good boy!" exclaimed the farmer patting him on the shoulder. "Those feelings do you great honour, and to show you my approval I shall let you free so that you can return home."

And he removed the dog collar from Pinocchio's neck.

*Pinocchio mourns the death
of the beautiful girl with the
raven-coloured hair. Then he
meets a dove who takes him to
the seashore, where he throws himself
into the water to go to the help of his
father, Geppetto.*

As soon as Pinocchio was free of the heavy and humiliating collar around his neck, he began to hurry through the fields, and did not stop for a minute until he had again reached the highway which would take him to the Fairy's house.

As he went along the road he looked at the plain below and was able to make out with his bare eyes the wood where he had been unlucky enough to meet the fox and the cat. He saw among the trees the top of the Great Oak on which he had been left hanging by the neck. But although he looked all about he was not able to see the little house belonging to the Fairy with the raven-coloured hair.

Then he thought of all kinds of sad things that might have happened, and began to run with all the strength that was left in his legs. In a few minutes he found himself in the meadow where at one time the little white house had stood, but it was no longer there.

Instead there was a small white stone of marble on which could be read in large letters these sad words:

HERE LIES THE YOUNG GIRL
WITH THE RAVEN-COLOURED HAIR
WHO DIED FROM GRIEF
WHEN ABANDONED BY HER LITTLE BROTHER
PINOCCHIO.

I leave it to you to think how the puppet felt when he read these words letter by letter. He knelt down and covered the little white gravestone with a million kisses. He burst out crying and he cried all night. On the following morning, when day came, he was still crying although his eyes had no more tears in them, and his cries and sobs were so heart-rending and distressing that all the little hills around repeated the echo. And while he was crying he said, "Oh my good little Fairy, why are you dead? Why am not I dead instead of you? I've always been so bad while you were so good. And my father, where is he? Oh my little Fairy, tell me where I can find him so that I can be with him always and never leave him again—never, never again! Oh my little Fairy, tell me it is not true that you are dead! If you really love me, if you love your little brother, please live again . . . come back to life, as you were before! Doesn't it make you unhappy to see me alone and deserted by everyone? If the highwaymen come again, if they hang me again to the bough of the tree, this time I shall die for good. What shall I do here alone in this world? Now that I have lost you and my father, who will give me something to eat? Where shall I go to sleep at night? Who will make a new little jacket for me? Oh it would have been better, a hundred times better, if I had died. Yes I want to die! Oh! Oh! Oh!"

And while he went on in this desperate way, he tried to pull out his hair, but his hair was made of wood and it was quite impossible to grab it between his fingers.

Meanwhile, a large dove flew by overhead and paused for a moment with its wings outstretched. It cried out to him from a great height, "What are you doing down there, my child?"

"Don't you see I am crying?" said Pinocchio, lifting his head towards the voice, and rubbing his eyes with the sleeve of his jacket.

The dove cried out again, "Do you know among

your friends, by any chance, a puppet that has the name Pinocchio?"

"Pinocchio? Did you say Pinocchio?" repeated the puppet, jumping quickly to his feet. "I am Pinocchio."

The dove, at this reply, came straight down and landed on the ground. He was bigger than a turkey.

"Do you know Geppetto too?" he asked the puppet.

"Do I know him? He is my father! Have you perhaps spoken to him about me? Can you lead me to him? Is he still alive? Answer me for goodness sake, is he still alive?"

'I left him three days ago on the seashore."

"What was he doing?"

"He was building himself a little boat to cross the ocean. That poor man has been travelling the world in search of you for more than four months. When he could not find you, he took it into his head to search for you in the distant lands of the new world."

"How far is it from here to the seashore?"

"More than a thousand miles."

"A thousand miles? Oh my dear dove, how lucky you are to have wings!"

"If you want to come, I can carry you."

"How?"

"On my back. Do you weigh much?"

"Weigh much? No. I am as light as a feather."

Without saying another word, Pinocchio jumped onto the back of the dove and put a leg on either side as if he were a horseman. He called out happily, "Giddyup, giddyup, my dear little horse. I want to arrive quickly!"

The dove took to the air and in a few minutes they had flown so high that they almost touched the clouds. The puppet thought he would like to look down from this great height, but when he did so he became very afraid, and was so dizzy that, to avoid falling, he had to embrace the neck of his feathered horse more tightly with his arms.

They flew all day, and towards the evening the dove said, "I am very thirsty!"

"And I am very hungry!" added Pinocchio.

"Let us stop at a loft in a few minutes and after that we shall set off again, so that tomorrow morning we shall reach the seashore."

They entered a deserted loft where there was only a small basin filled with water and a little basket full of grass and seeds. Up until that time the puppet had never been able to eat grass or seeds. Just the thought of them made him feel sick in the stomach. But that evening he ate them until he was full and when he had almost finished he turned to the dove and said, "I would never have believed that grass and seeds could be so good."

"It is necessary to realize, my dear boy," answered the dove, "that when we are hungry and it is a question of eating or not eating, grass and seeds can seem the best food in the world. Hunger is never dainty in eating habits!"

They had another quick snack, made themselves ready to travel again, and away!

Next morning they arrived at the seashore.

The dove set Pinocchio on the ground and, because he did not wish in the least to be thanked for his good action, he took off immediately and disappeared.

The seashore was full of people who were shouting and pointing out to sea.

"What has happened?" Pinocchio asked an old lady.

"An old man has lost his son and has set out in a small boat to look for him on the other side of the ocean. But the sea is so rough today that the small boat is just about to sink."

"Where is the boat?"

"There it is, straight out there," said the old lady pointing towards a tiny boat which, seen from such a distance, looked like a nutshell with a very small man in it.

Pinocchio followed her direction and after searching for some time he let out a sharp cry, "It's my father! It's my father!"

Meanwhile the little boat, battered by the fury of the waves, disappeared among the great rollers and then came up and managed to keep afloat.

Pinocchio stood right on the top of a high rock and kept on calling to his father by name and making signs with his hands, and waving his handkerchief and his cap.

It seemed that Geppetto, although he was so far away from the shore, recognized his son, because he also lifted his beret and waved. He gave many signals to make Pinocchio understand that he would gladly have come back but the seas were so large that he was prevented from doing so.

All of a sudden a terrible wave poured over him and the boat disappeared. The people on the shore waited for the boat to float again but this time they did not see it.

"Poor man!" said all the fishermen who had collected on the shore, and muttering a prayer in low voices they turned to go back to their homes. Suddenly they heard a loud cry, and turning around they saw a small boy throw himself into the seas from the top of a rock. They heard him call out, "I want to save my father!"

Because he was made of wood, Pinocchio floated easily and swam like a fish. At one moment he disappeared under the water, carried down by the force of a wave, and at the next he reappeared, with a leg or arm showing, at a great distance from the shore. At last he was lost to sight and they saw him no more.

"Poor boy!" said the fishermen who had grouped on the shore, and muttering a prayer in low voices they returned to their homes.

CHAPTER 24

Pinocchio arrives at the Island of the Busy Bees and meets the Fairy.

Pinocchio swam on and on all night in the hope of saving his poor father. And what a horrible night that was! It rained and hailed, and thundered, and the lightning made it seem like day.

When morning came, he managed to see a long strip of land not far away. It was an island standing on its own in the sea.

He tried his hardest to reach the shore of the island but it was useless. The waves ran together, heaped up, and tumbled down, taking him with them as if he had been a twig or a piece of straw. At length, by good luck, a very large wave picked him up and hurled him heavily on the sand of the beach. He was thrown down so hard that all his ribs and joints creaked, but he made himself feel better by saying, "At last it's all over and I'm safe!"

Meanwhile the sky was slowly becoming clearer. The sun shone brightly and the sea became calm and smooth as oil.

The puppet spread out his clothes to dry in the sun and began to look around in the hope of seeing on that immense space of water the small boat with a small man in it. But after some time he still saw nothing except the sky, the sea, and the sails of a ship so far away that it looked like a fly.

"I wonder what on earth they call this island," he said to himself. "I wonder if it is inhabited by kind people. Or should I rather say, people who are not fond of hanging children from the boughs of trees. But who am I going to ask? There's no one in sight."

The thought of finding himself completely alone in some large, uninhabited country made him so unhappy that he gradually began to cry. All of a sudden he noticed, not far from the shore, a large fish which went very calmly about its own business with its head out of the water.

The little puppet did not know how to call it by name, so he cried out in a loud voice, "Hey, Mr Fish, would you be kind enough to spare me a word?"

"Even two words," answered the fish, who was a very kind and pleasant dolphin. There were not many like him in all the seas of the world.

"Would you be kind enough to tell me if this island is a place where people are able to eat without danger of being eaten?"

"I am quite sure it is," replied the dolphin. "Indeed you will find some of the people not far from here."

"Which way should I go?"

"You ought to take that path on the left and simply follow your nose. You cannot mistake it."

"Please tell me another thing. In your journeys through the sea all day and all night, I don't suppose you have come across a very small boat with my father in it?"

"And who is your father?"

"He is the best father in the world, just as I am the worst son that you would ever find."

"With the storm that took place last night," replied the dolphin, "the little boat would have been sunk."

"And my father?"

"By now he will have been swallowed by the terrible Sea Monster that has been spreading slaughter and misery in these waters for some days."

"And is this Sea Monster so very big?" asked Pinocchio, who was already beginning to tremble with fear.

"Is he big?" replied the dolphin. "Perhaps I can give you some idea of his size if I tell you that he is as big as a five storey house and that his mouth is so wide and deep that a train could easily pass down it at full steam."

"Oh dear!" cried the puppet very much afraid. He dressed himself in a great hurry and turned to the dolphin and said, "Goodbye Mr Fish. Excuse me if I have caused you any inconvenience, and a thousand thanks for your kindness."

Then he quickly entered the little path and began to walk at a fast pace, so fast that he was almost running. Every little noise frightened him, and he kept looking behind because he was afraid of being followed by the terrible Sea Monster that was as large as a five storey house and could hold a train in its mouth.

After following the path for half an hour he arrived at a small town called the town of the Busy Bees. The road was full of persons who were running hither and thither about their business, all of them working. Everyone had something to do. Not a single lazy or idle person was to be seen.

"This is not the country for me!" said that good-for-nothing Pinocchio, "I was not born for work!"

By now he was feeling very hungry because it was forty-eight hours since he had eaten anything. He had not even had a feed of grass and seeds in that time.

What was he to do?

There were only two ways for him to eat: either to do a little work, or to beg a few cents or a mouthful of bread.

He was ashamed to ask for charity because his father had always told him that charity can only be sought by the old or the sick. The truly poor people in this world deserve pity and help. These are the people who, because of age or sickness, are unable to gain bread from the work of their own hands. All the rest are obliged to work, and if they do not work they go hungry, and so much the worse for them.

In the meantime a man passed along the road. He was dripping with sweat and out of breath, for he was pulling along, with great effort, two carts full of coal.

Pinocchio could see by his face that he was a good man. He went up to him and, lowering his eyes with shame, said in a quiet voice, "Would you do me the charity of giving me a cent; I feel as though I am dying of hunger?"

"Not just one cent," replied the man, "but four of them, if you will help me to pull home these two carts full of coal."

"You surprise me!" replied the puppet, almost taking offence. "You might like to know that I am not a donkey. I have never pulled carts!"

"So much the better for you," replied the coalman. "However, my boy, if you really feel that you are dying from hunger you should eat two slices of your pride, and mind that you do not get indigestion."

A few minutes later a bricklayer with a bucketful of mortar on his shoulders passed by.

"Kind sir, would you do me the charity of giving a cent to a poor boy who is starving?"

"Gladly. Come with me and carry some mortar," replied the bricklayer, "and instead of a cent I will give you five."

"But the mortar is heavy," answered Pinocchio. "And I do not want to tire myself."

"If you do not want to tire yourself, my boy, then amuse yourself by being hungry.

In less than half an hour some twenty persons passed by, and Pinocchio asked a little charity of each but all replied, "Aren't you ashamed? Instead of being a loafer on the road, you should do a little work and learn to earn your bread."

At length a young lady passed by carrying two jugs of water. "Good day, young lady. Would you let me have a sip from your jug?" asked Pinocchio, who was burning with thirst.

"Have a good drink, my boy," said the young lady, putting the jugs on the ground.

When Pinocchio had taken a deep drink he mumbled in a low voice, drying his mouth, "My thirst is quenched at last. I wish I could do the same for my hunger."

The young lady replied, "If you will help me to carry home one of these jugs of water I will give you a large slice of bread."

Pinocchio looked at the jug and did not say yes or no.

"And with the bread I will give you a plate of cauliflower, seasoned with oil and vinegar," added the young lady.

Pinocchio had another look at the jug and did not say yes or no.

"With the cauliflower I will give you some lovely sugared almonds sweetened with syrup."

At this last temptation, Pinocchio could not resist. He said in a firm voice, "Very well. I will carry one of the jugs to your house."

The jug was very heavy and the puppet did not have the strength to carry it with his hands, so he was forced to carry it on his head. When they arrived at the house the good young lady made Pinocchio sit down at a little table which was laid out for a meal and put before him the bread, the seasoned cauliflower, and the sugared almonds. Pinocchio did not eat the food; he devoured it! His stomach felt like a district that had been left empty and uninhabited for five months.

Little by little the sharp feeling of hunger went away. Then he lifted his head to thank the young lady, but he had hardly fixed his eyes on her before he gave a very long "Ohhh" of wonder and sat quite still, his eyes wide open, his fork in the air, and his mouth full of bread and cauliflower.

"What is the matter with you?" said the young lady laughing.

The puppet stuttered, "It is . . . it is . . . it is . . . you are so similar . . . you remind me . . . yes, yes, yes! The same voice, the same eyes, the same hair. Yes, yes, yes. You have the same raven-coloured hair, just like her—Oh my Fairy, my Fairy, tell me that it's you, really you. Don't make me cry any longer. If only you knew how much I have cried, how much I have suffered!"

In saying this Pinocchio began to cry again, and he threw his arms around that mysterious young lady.

CHAPTER 25

Pinocchio promises the Fairy that he will be good and will study because he is tired of being a puppet and wants to become a clever boy.

The good young lady said at first that she was not the little Fairy with the raven-coloured hair but then, seeing that she was discovered, and not wanting to keep Pinocchio in doubt any longer, she admitted who she was and said to him, "You rascal of a puppet! How did you ever manage to recognize me?"

"It is because I love you so much. That is how I knew."

"Do you remember how you left me as a girl? And now you find me as a woman. I've grown up so much that I could almost be your mother."

"I love you so much, so very much, that instead of 'little sister' I shall call you my mother. I have always longed to have a mother like all the other boys! But how did you ever manage to grow so quickly?"

"It's a secret."

"Teach it to me; I should like to grow a little myself. Haven't you noticed? I have always remained a little fellow."

"But you cannot grow," replied the Fairy.

"Why?"

"Because puppets never grow. They are born puppets, they live puppets, and they die puppets."

"Oh, I am tired of being a puppet," cried Pinocchio giving himself a rap on the head. "Oh, how I should like to grow into a man like all the other boys."

"And you will become one if you learn how to deserve it."

"Really? How could I ever deserve it?"

"It's a very simple thing. Accustom yourself to being a good little boy."

"Oh, aren't I one?"

"I am afraid not! The good boys are obedient, and you . . ."

"And I never obey."

"The good boys love study and work, and you . . ."

"And I instead am a lazy vagabond from one year's end to the other."

"The good boys always speak the truth."

"And I always speak lies."

"The good boys gladly go to school."

"And I hate going to school. But from today I want to change my way of life."

"Do you promise me that?"

"I promise it. I want to become a real boy and also I want to make my father happy. Oh, where could my poor father be at this moment?"

"I do not know."

"Will I ever have the good fortune of seeing him again and embracing him?"

"I think so. Yes, I am sure of it."

At this reply the happiness of Pinocchio was so great that he took the Fairy's hands and kissed them again and again. He was almost beside himself with joy. Then lifting his face to her lovingly he asked, "My dear mother, is it true that you are not dead?"

"It seems not," replied the Fairy, laughing.

"If you only knew how sad and miserable I felt when I read HERE LIES . . ."

"I know, and that is why I have pardoned you. The sincerity of your sorrow made me realize that you have a good heart, and for boys with a good heart, even if they are rascals and have become accustomed to acting badly, there is always some hope. There is always a chance that they will get on to the right path again. That is why I have come here to look after you. I will be your mother."

"Oh how wonderful!" cried Pinocchio jumping with happiness.

"You will obey me and will always do what I tell you?"

"Gladly, gladly, gladly!"

"From tomorrow," added the Fairy, "you will begin by going to school."

Pinocchio suddenly became a little less cheerful.

"Then you will choose for yourself a trade or craft." Pinocchio became serious.

"What are you mumbling between your teeth?" asked the Fairy in a hurt tone.

"I was saying," muttered the puppet in a low voice, "that it seems to me a little late for going to school."

"Oh no indeed! Always keep in mind that for teaching yourself things and for learning it is never too late."

"But I do not want to learn a trade or craft."

"Why?"

"Because I find work too tiring."

"My boy," said the Fairy, "people who say that nearly always finish up either in prison or in hospital. You must believe me when I tell you that a man may be born rich or poor, but in this world he is obliged to do something. He must keep himself busy; he must work. It is too bad for those who let themselves become idle! Laziness is a very nasty sickness, and it is necessary to cure it quickly among children. If not, when they are grown up it will never be cured."

These last words made a deep impression on Pinocchio, and he held up his head with determination and said to the Fairy, "I'll study, I'll work, I'll do everything that you tell me, because I've grown tired of a puppet's life and I want to become a real boy. You promised me that. It is true, isn't it?"

"I promised you that, and now it depends on you."

CHAPTER 26

Pinocchio goes with his school-mates to the seashore to see the terrible Sea Monster.

Next day Pinocchio went to the local school.

You can imagine how those rascals of school children behaved when they saw a puppet come into the classroom. There was such a burst of laughter that it seemed as though it would never stop. Everyone played a different trick on him. One boy grabbed his cap, another pulled his little jacket from behind, another tried to paint great moustaches under his nose, and another even dared to tie thin wires to his feet and hands in order to make him dance.

At first Pinocchio took no notice and drew away. But finally he began to lose his patience. He turned on those who were bullying him and making fun of him and said sternly, "Now see here, boys, I have not come here to be your clown. I respect you and I want to be respected by you."

"What a clever chap! You talk like a school book!" shouted some of those young rascals, rolling on the floor and laughing foolishly. Another boy, cheekier than the others, put out his hand with the idea of catching the puppet by the end of his nose. But he was not quick enough, because Pinocchio stretched out under the table and gave the boy a kick in the shins.

"Ouch! What hard feet!" shouted the boy, rubbing the bruise that the puppet had made.

"And what elbows! Even harder than the feet!" said another rude boy, who had received an elbow in the stomach.

After the kick and the elbow Pinocchio very quickly received the respect he demanded, and the boys in the school became his friends. They all knew he was a lad who would stand up for himself.

The schoolmaster praised him often because he listened in class, he did his work cheerfully, and he was clever. He was always the first into school in the morning, and always the last to rise to his feet when school was finished. His only fault was that he kept bad company. He was friendly with most of the naughty children who did not like to study and who were often in trouble.

The master warned him every day, and the good Fairy said to him over and over again, "Watch out, Pinocchio! Those companions of yours will finish up sooner or later with making you lose your love of study and perhaps with leading you into some very bad disgrace."

"There is no danger," answered the puppet, shrugging his shoulders and tapping his finger on the middle of his forehead as if to say, "There is lots of good sense in here!"

Then one fine day, while he was walking towards school, he met a group of his usual friends who were coming the other way, and they said to him, "Have you heard the big news?"

"No."

"The Sea Monster has been noticed in the sea near here. He is as big as a mountain."

"Really? That must be the same Sea Monster that sank my poor father's boat."

"We're going down to the beach to see him. Are you coming along?"

"No, not me. I'm going to school."

"What's the use of school? We can always go to

school tomorrow. One lesson more or less won't matter to donkeys like us."

"But what will the teacher say?"

"Let the teacher say what he likes. He's paid to grumble at us all day."

"And what about my mother?"

"Mothers never know anything," replied those rascals.

"Do you know what I'll do?" said Pinocchio. "I want to see the Sea Monster for certain reasons of my own, but I'll go after school."

"Silly fellow!" replied one of the gang. "Do you think that a fish of that size will wait on your convenience? As soon as he gets tired of these parts he will head off and you'll be lucky to see him again.

"How long does it take to get to the seashore?" asked the puppet.

"We will be there and back in an hour."

"Come on then, and anyone who likes can have a race with me," cried Pinocchio.

This was the signal they had been waiting for. The gang of rascals started to run through the fields with their books and cases under their arms. Pinocchio kept in front. He seemed to have wings on his feet.

He looked back from time to time and made fun of his companions, who kept a good distance behind. He laughed when he saw them panting, out of breath and dusty, with their tongues hanging out. The unlucky puppet did not know at that moment just what terrors and what horrible misfortunes he was running to meet!

CHAPTER 27

A great fight takes place between Pinocchio and his school-mates. One of them is wounded and Pinocchio is arrested by the police.

When he arrived at the seashore Pinocchio immediately had a long look out to sea but he saw no sign of the Sea Monster. The sea was as smooth as a great mirror.

"Where is the Sea Monster?" he asked, turning towards his friends.

"He must have gone to breakfast," replied one of them, laughing.

"Or perhaps he has gone to bed for a little sleep," added another boy, laughing even more loudly.

Pinocchio knew from these joking replies and silly laughs that his schoolmates had played a nasty joke on him. He said to them angrily,

"Well, so this is how it goes! Just why have you decided to tell me this little story about the Sea Monster?"

"There's a good reason!" those young rascals replied in chorus.

"And what is it?"

"It was to make you miss school and come with us. Aren't you ashamed of studying as much as you do?"

"And if I wish to study, what has that to do with you?"

"It has a lot to do with us because it means we cut a poor figure with the teacher."

"Why?"

102

"Because students who study hard always make the others, like us, who do not want to study, look lazy by comparison. And we do not like to cut a poor figure. We have our pride, too!"

"And what do you think I should do to satisfy you?"

"You, too, ought to grow tired of school, the lessons, and the teacher, which are our three great enemies."

"And if I choose to continue to study?"

"We will not have anything more to do with you, and at the first opportunity we will make you pay for it!"

"To tell you the truth, you almost make me laugh," said the puppet with a shake of the head.

"Hey, Pinocchio!" cried the biggest of the boys, going up to him and looking right into his face. "Don't try to bully us and show off! Because if you aren't afraid of us, we certainly aren't afraid of you! Remember that you are alone and there are seven of us."

"Like the seven deadly sins!" said Pinocchio with a loud laugh.

"Did you hear what he said? He insulted all of us! He called us the seven deadly sins!"

"Look here, Pinocchio! You must apologize for that. If you don't, you'll be sorry for it!"

"Cuckoo!" said the puppet, putting his finger to his nose to show just what he thought of them.

"I warned you, Pinocchio. You'll come off worst!"

"Cuckoo!"

"Don't be such a donkey!"

"Cuckoo!"

"You'll be going home with a broken nose!"

"Cuckoo!"

"I'll 'cuckoo' you!" cried the most hot-tempered of the gang. "Take this on account! Eat it for dinner this evening!"

And as he said this, he aimed a punch at Pinocchio's head.

But Pinocchio made it tit-for-tat. The puppet was expecting the blow, and he replied with another one.

In a moment the fight really began and everyone joined in.

Although Pinocchio was on his own he defended himself like a hero. He worked so well with those feet of very hard wood that he always kept his enemies at a respectable distance. Whenever his feet made contact they never failed to leave a good bruise to be remembered by.

The boys soon became annoyed because they could not deal with the puppet at close range, so instead they stood back and threw things at him. They loosened the straps around their school books and began to hurl at Pinocchio their spellers, grammar books, histories, readers, and exercise books. But the puppet had a quick and cunning eye and he always ducked in time, with the result that the books passed over his head and fell into the sea.

Just imagine the fish! They thought that these books were food to be eaten and they gathered around in shoals to enjoy them, but after swallowing a few pages or some binding they spat them out at once, and made wry faces as if to say "This isn't food for us! We are used to much better!"

The fight was growing fiercer and fiercer when a large crab, who had come out of the water and was slowly clawing his way up the shore, cried out with a voice that sounded like a trombone suffering from a cold, "Stop that, you young rascals! You should know better! These cruel wars among boys never come to any good. They always end with a serious accident!"

Poor Mr Crab! It was just as if he had preached to the wind. Indeed that naughty lad, Pinocchio, turning behind to give him a surly look, said rudely, "Be quiet you tedious old crab! You'd do better to suck some throat lozenges for that sore throat of yours. Or you might go to bed and try to sweat it out!"

Just at that moment the other boys, who had now thrown away all their own books, looked around for the books belonging to the puppet. They took charge of them in less time than it takes to say.

Among these books, there was one with a very thick cover completely bound in leather. It was a Treatise of Arithmetic, and you can just imagine how heavy that would be!

One of those young rogues snatched up this volume, took aim at Pinocchio's head, and hurled the book with all the force that he had in his arm. But instead of hitting the puppet, he caught the head of one of his own companions, who went as white as a sheet and said only, "Oh, mummy, help me . . . I am dying!" Then he fell down on the sand.

At the sight of that little figure, apparently dead, the other lads became afraid and ran away as fast as their legs would carry them. In a few minutes there was not one to be seen.

Pinocchio remained there however, and although he felt half dead from sorrow and fear, he ran to dip his handkerchief in the sea and began to bathe the temple of his poor little school-mate. He wept and cried out desperately, and called the boy by name, saying, "Eugene! My poor little Eugene! Open your eyes and look at me! Why don't you answer? It wasn't me who did this awful thing to you, believe me! Open your eyes Eugene. . . . If you keep your eyes closed, I will die too. . . . Oh dear! How am I ever going to return home? I couldn't face my good mother. What am I going to do? Where shall I run away to? Where am I going to hide myself? Oh, how much better it would have been, how many thousand times better, if I had gone to school! Why did I listen to these companions who have been the ruin of me? And the teacher told me! And my mother repeated to me 'Watch out for those bad companions!' but I am obstinate and headstrong . . . I don't listen to anyone and I always go my own way! And then I am sorry for it. . . . And that is why, ever since I have been in the world, I have always been in

105

trouble. Oh dear! What will become of me? What will become of me? What will become of me? . . ."

Pinocchio continued to weep and cry out and beat his hand on his head, at the same time as he called the poor Eugene by name. Then quite suddenly he heard a muffled noise of steps approaching.

He turned around and saw two policemen.

"What are you doing there on the ground?" they asked Pinocchio.

"I'm helping my schoolmate."

"Is he badly hurt?"

"It seems so!"

"Worse than bad!" said one of the policemen, kneeling down and looking closely at Eugene. "This boy has been hit on the temple. Who did it?"

"Not me," blurted out the puppet who had hardly any breath left in his body.

"If it wasn't you, then who did hit him?"

"Not me," repeated Pinocchio.

"What was he hit with?"

"With this book."

The puppet picked up from the ground the Treatise of Arithmetic bound in leather and handed it to the policeman.

"Whose book is this?"

"Mine."

"Is it indeed? Well that's a coincidence! You can stand up at once and come along with us."

"But I . . ."

"Come along now!"

"But I am innocent . . ."

"Come along now!"

Before leaving, the policemen called to some fishermen who at that moment were passing by in their boat close to the shore. They said to them,

"We want you to look after this little boy who has been hit on the head. Take him to your house and care for him. We'll come back tomorrow to see him."

Then they placed Pinocchio between them and gave him orders like a soldier:

"Forward! Quick march! Come along now! No nonsense!"

The puppet did not wait for them to say it again. He began to walk with them along the path that led to the town. But the poor little fellow did not know whether he was in this world or the next. He seemed to be dreaming, and what an ugly dream! He was scared out of his wits. His eyes were seeing double; his legs trembled; his tongue was stuck to the roof of his mouth and he could not utter a single word. Suddenly another sorrow cut into the puppet's heart: he remembered that he would pass beneath the window of the good Fairy's house between the two policemen. He would much prefer to die.

They had already arrived at the outskirts of the town when a rough gust of wind lifted Pinocchio's little beret from his head and carried it ten yards away.

"If you will permit me," the puppet said to the policemen, "I will go and pick up my beret."

"Go along then, but be quick about it."

The puppet moved to pick up the beret but instead of putting it on his head he stuck it between his teeth and began to run at full speed towards the seashore. He went like a bullet out of a gun.

The policemen knew they would never catch him themselves, so they sent after him a large mastiff dog that had won first prize in all the dog races. Pinocchio ran, and the dog ran after him. All the people came to their windows and crowded into the street to see the end of this race. But they were not successful because the dog and Pinocchio lifted such a cloud of dust along the road that after a few minutes it was impossible to see anything.

During that headlong chase there was one terrible moment when Pinocchio believed himself lost. The mastiff, whose name was Alidoro, ran with such fury that he almost caught the puppet. Pinocchio heard behind him, not more than six inches away, the panting breath of the animal, and he could almost feel its hot blast on his back.

But he was now near the seashore. He sprinted across the sand and gave a great leap, like a frog, which landed him well out in the water. Alidoro wanted to stop but he was travelling too fast and went straight into the water. The unlucky dog did not know how to swim. He began to struggle with his paws to keep himself afloat but the more he struggled the more his head went under the water. When his head showed above the water the poor dog's eyes were rolling with fear. He barked and cried out, "I'm drowning! I'm drowning!"

"Serves you right!" cried Pinocchio from a distance. He could now see that he was safe from every danger.

"Help me, Pinocchio! Save me from dying!"

At this pleading cry the puppet, who deep down had a very good heart, began to feel sorry, and turning to the dog he said,

"If I save you, do you promise you won't bother me or chase me any more?"

"I promise, I promise! Hurry for heaven's sake, because if you delay another half a minute I'll be well and truly dead."

Pinocchio still hesitated a little, but then he remembered that his father had told him many times that he should never miss the chance to do a good deed. He swam to Alidoro, took him by the tail with two hands, and dragged him to the safety of the shore.

The poor dog could no longer support himself on his feet. He had swallowed so much salt water that he was puffed up like a balloon. The puppet did not want to take any chances with the mastiff so he dived again into the sea and swam well away from the shore. Then he cried out to the friend he had saved,

"Goodbye Alidoro! Have a good trip home and give my best wishes to your family."

"Goodbye, Pinocchio," answered the dog. "A thousand thanks for saving me from death. You have done me a good turn and in this life one good turn deserves another. I shall not forget when I have a chance to help you."

Pinocchio kept on swimming but stayed close to the shore. At last he seemed to have arrived at a safe place. He looked each way along the shore and saw on the rocks a kind of cave from which came a long plume of smoke.

"There must be a fire in that cave," he said to himself. "That's good! I'll go and dry myself and warm up a little. . . . And then? . . . And then we shall see what we shall see."

Having made this resolution he swam close to the rocks, but when he was going to pull himself up he felt something under the water that rose up and up and up, and carried him through the air.

He tried to get away but it was too late, because to his great amazement he found himself closed in by a large net in the middle of a great mass of fish of every kind and size that were threshing about and struggling madly for dear life.

At the same time he saw outside the cave a fisherman who was very ugly indeed. He looked like some kind of strange sea creature. Instead of hair he had on his head a very thick tuft of green seaweed; the skin of his body was green, his eyes were green, his very long beard was green, and it descended right down to the ground. He looked like a great green lizard standing upright on its two back feet.

When the fisherman had drawn the net in from the sea he cried out happily,

"Blessed providence! Today I shall have a good belly-ful of fish again!"

"It's just as well that I'm not a fish!" Pinocchio said to himself, getting a little courage back. The net full of fish was carried inside the cave. It was dark and smoky, and in the middle a great pan of oil was sizzling noisily, giving out a smell of burning grease that was enough to take away your breath.

"Now let's see what fish we have taken!" said the green fisherman, and plunging into the net an enormous hand, almost as large as a spade, he drew out a handful of mullet.

"What good mullet!" he cried, looking at them and smelling them with pleasure. And after having smelt them he threw them into an empty tub. He did this again and again until he had taken out all the fish. His mouth watered as he gloated over his catch, and he said, "What good whiting! What exquisite trout! How delici-ous these flounder are! What tasty ling fish! What beautiful little anchovies!"

The whiting, the trout, the flounder, the ling, and the anchovies all went into the tub in a heap to keep the mullet company.

At last only Pinocchio remained in the net. The fisherman pulled him out and scratched his head with wonder. He opened wide his green eyes and said,

"What species of fish is this? I don't recall ever having eaten fish that looked like this!"

He looked at it carefully, turning it over and over. At last he said,

"I understand; it must be a crab."

Pinocchio was most upset at being mistaken for a crab, and said resentfully,

"I certainly am not a crab, and please be careful how you handle me! If you would really like to know, I am a puppet."

"A puppet?" replied the fisherman. "To tell the truth, the puppet-fish is a new one on me! So much the better. I'll eat you all the more gladly."

"Eat me? But don't you understand that I am not a fish? Can't you hear me speak, and don't you notice how I think with my brain just like you?"

"That's very true," said the fisherman, "and since I see that you are a fish that has the good fortune to be able to speak and think like me, I shall extend all the more respect to you."

"And what respect will that be?"

"As a sign of my friendship and high regard I shall leave to you the choice of the way in which you would like to be cooked. Do you wish to be fried in oil, or would you prefer to be baked in tomato sauce?"

"To be truthful," answered the puppet, "if I have to choose I would prefer rather to be let free so that I can return home."

"You must be joking. Do you think that I will miss the chance of trying such a rare fish? A puppet-fish does not turn up every day in these seas. Just leave it to me! I shall fry you in oil along with all the other fish, and you shall be quite happy with it. It is always a consolation to be fried in company."

On hearing this the unhappy Pinocchio began to cry and scream and beg for mercy. "Oh how much better it would have been if I had gone to school!" he said. "I listened to bad companions, and now I am paying for it! Oh! Oh! Oh!"

He wriggled like an eel and tried very hard to squirm

out of the fisherman's fingers. The green fisherman picked up a long strip of reed and bound the puppet by the hands and feet like a sausage, and threw him into the tub with the other fish.

Then he took out a large wooden bowl full of flour and began to dip all the fish in it. As he put flour over them one by one he threw them into the pan of oil to fry.

The first ones to dance around in the boiling oil were the poor whiting, then it was the turn of the ling, the mullet, the flounder, the anchovy, and last of all it was Pinocchio's turn. When the puppet saw himself so close to death (and what an ugly death!) he was taken by such a fit of trembling and felt so afraid that he had neither voice nor breath to plead for help.

The poor boy begged with his eyes, but the green fisherman, taking no notice at all, rolled him five or six times in the flour. He was covered so well from head to foot that he looked like a puppet made of chalk. Then the fisherman took him by the head and . . .

CHAPTER 29

Pinocchio returns to the house of the Fairy, who promises him that next day he will no longer be a puppet but will become a real boy. A feast is prepared to celebrate this great occasion.

When the fisherman was just on the point of throwing Pinocchio into the pan, a large dog entered the cave.

He had been drawn there by the smell of frying fish.

"Clear out!" cried the fisherman, threatening the dog with one hand while he held the flour-covered puppet in the other.

But the poor dog was very hungry, and he wagged his tail and growled as if to say,

"Give me a mouthful of fried fish and I will leave you in peace."

"Clear out, I tell you!" repeated the fisherman, and raised his leg to give the dog a kick.

But the dog, who was very hungry indeed, and was not used to being pushed around in this way, turned and snarled at the fisherman, showing his sharp fangs.

Just then a very faint voice said,

"Save me Alidoro! If you do not save me I shall be fried!"

The dog recognized the voice of Pinocchio at once and could hardly believe that the voice had come out of the floury lump that the fisherman was holding in his hand.

He hesitated for a moment, then leapt up from the ground, grasped that floury lump in his mouth and, holding it lightly between his teeth, he ran out of the cave and was gone like a flash of lightning.

The fisherman was very angry at losing the fish that he was so keen to eat, and began to run after the dog. But he had taken only a few steps when he had a fit of coughing and had to turn back.

Meanwhile Alidoro had reached the path that led to the town. There he stopped and put his friend Pinocchio gently down on the ground.

"How can I ever thank you enough?" said the puppet.

"There is no need," replied the dog. "You saved me and I am returning the favour. As the saying goes 'in this life one good turn deserves another'."

"But how did you ever come to turn up in that cave?"

"I was stretched out on the shore there, more dead than alive, when the smell of frying fish came to me on the wind. That smell gave me an appetite, so I followed it up. If I had arrived just one minute later . . . !"

"Don't say it!" cried Pinocchio who was still trembling from fear. "Don't say it! If you had arrived a minute later, by now I would be well and truly fried, eaten, and digested. Ugh! It gives me the shivers just to think of it!"

Alidoro laughed and held out his right paw. The puppet pressed it firmly as a sign of strong friendship, and they parted.

The dog took the road home and Pinocchio, left alone, went to a hut a short distance away and spoke to an old man who was sitting outside warming himself in the sun.

"Tell me, kind sir, do you know anything of an unfortunate little boy who was wounded in the head? His name was Eugene."

"The boy was brought home by some fishermen who live in this hut. . . ."

"And now he is dead?" interrupted Pinocchio with great sorrow.

"No! He is alive and has now returned to his own home."

"Really and truly?" shouted the puppet jumping with

114

happiness. "Then the wound was not serious?"

"No, but it could have been very serious, even fatal," answered the old man, "because someone threw at his head a heavy book bound in leather."

"Who threw it?"

"One of his schoolmates—a certain Pinocchio. . . ."

"And who is this Pinocchio?" asked the puppet, pretending not to know who the man was talking about.

"They say that he is a bad lad, a vagabond, a wild fellow. . . ."

"Lies! All lies!"

"Do you know this Pinocchio?"

"By sight," answered the puppet.

"And what is your opinion of him?"

"He seems to me a very good son, full of the desire to study, obedient, affectionate to his father and his family. . . ."

While the puppet was telling all these new lies, he noticed that his nose had grown six inches. Then, suddenly afraid, he began to cry out,

"Please forget what I have just said to you about Pinocchio, because I know him very well and I can assure you that he really is a bad lad, a disobedient boy, and a ne'er-do-well, who instead of going to school runs away with his schoolmates and gets up to mischief."

He had no sooner said these words than his nose shrank and returned to its natural size.

"Tell me, why have you turned so white?" the old man asked him suddenly.

"Well, you see . . . I brushed against a wall which was freshly painted," answered the puppet, ashamed to confess that he had been dipped in flour like a fish that is going to be fried in a pan.

"I notice you're not wearing a coat, or shoes, or cap. Haven't you got any?"

"I met some thieves who stole them. I don't suppose, old fellow, that by any chance you have an old coat which I could wear until I reach home?"

"My boy, I am afraid that all I can offer you is a little sack which I use for beans. If you want to take it, here is is."

Pinocchio took the empty bean sack gladly, and made holes in the end for his head and arms. Then he put it on like a shirt, and dressed in that way he headed towards the town.

He felt nervous as he walked along the road, and finally took one step backwards for every two steps forward. He said to himself as he went along,

"How am I going to face my good Fairy? What will she say when she sees me? Will she pardon me for this second piece of mischief? I am afraid that she won't excuse it. Oh, she won't excuse it for certain. . . . It serves me right because I'm a rascal who always promises to behave better next time and never does!"

He arrived at the village after dark, and because it was a stormy night, with rain pelting down, he went straight to the house of the Fairy, determined to knock at the door and be let in.

But when he got there he felt his courage fail him and instead of knocking he went away. He retreated about twenty paces, then approached the door a second time, and still could not get up enough courage. He approached a third time and still could not knock. The fourth time, still trembling, he took the iron knocker in his hand and gave it a little tap.

He waited and waited, and finally after half an hour a window opened on the top floor (it was a house of four storeys) and Pinocchio saw a large snail put out its head with a small light on top. It said,

"Who is it at this hour?"

"Is the Fairy home?"

"The Fairy is asleep and does not want to be woken. But who are you . . . ?"

"It's me!"

"Who is me?"

"Pinocchio!"

"Who is Pinocchio?"

"The puppet who lives in the house with the Fairy."

"Oh I see," answered the snail. "Wait there for me - while I come down and I will open the door for you at once."

"Hurry up for heaven's sake; I'm dying of cold."

"My boy, I am a snail, and snails never hurry."

An hour passed by, then two hours, and the door still was not opened.

Pinocchio, who was soaked through, trembled with cold and fear. He gathered up his courage and knocked a second time, more strongly than before.

At this second knock a window opened on the next floor down, and the same snail put its head out.

"Beautiful little snail," cried the puppet from the street, "I have been waiting for two hours, and on a terrible night like this two hours seems longer than two years. Please hurry for heaven's sake."

That little beast, who was all peace and calmness, replied from the window, "My boy, I am a snail, and snails never hurry." And she closed the window.

Time passed and midnight sounded, then one o'clock, then two o'clock, and still the door was not opened.

Pinocchio finally lost his patience. He grasped the knocker angrily and gave it a great blow which echoed all through the building, but the knocker, which was made of iron, suddenly became an eel which squirmed out of his hands and disappeared in the overflowing gutter in the middle of the street.

"We'll see who's going to win!" cried the puppet, more angry than ever. "Since the knocker has disappeared I'll knock with my feet."

He drew back his foot and placed a hard kick right in the middle of the door. The blow was so strong that his foot went right through the wood, and when the puppet tried to take it back through the hole he could not do so because the foot was stuck inside as though it were a nail that had been driven in.

Just picture to yourself that poor little Pinocchio! He had to pass all the rest of the night with one foot on the ground and the other one up in the air.

Next morning, at the break of day, the door finally opened. That brave little beast of a snail had taken only nine hours to descend from the fourth floor to the street.

"What are you doing with your foot stuck in the door?" she asked, laughing at the puppet.

"It was an accident. I say, my dear little snail, could you possibly manage to free me from this awkward position?"

"My boy, that will require a carpenter and I have never learned the trade of carpentry."

"Please beg the Fairy to come and help me."

"The Fairy is asleep and does not want to be woken."

"But what do you expect me to do now that I am stuck like a nail? I'll be here all day in this door."

"Amuse yourself by counting the ants that pass by on the street."

"At least bring me something to eat; I'm almost done!"

"Immediately!" said the snail.

And indeed after three and a half hours Pinocchio saw her return with a silver tray on her head. On the tray there was a loaf of bread, a roast chicken, and four ripe apricots.

"Here is the breakfast that the Fairy has sent you," said the snail.

At the sight of this tasty meal the puppet felt a good deal better. But how great was his disappointment when he began to eat and found that the bread was made of chalk, the chicken was made of cardboard, and the four apricots were made of coloured plaster.

He wanted to cry, he wanted to stamp his feet and beat his hands on something, he wanted to throw away the tray and everything on it, but instead, perhaps because of his great sorrow and the emptiness of his stomach, he fell down in a faint.

When he came to himself again he was lying on a couch and the Fairy was beside him.

"I pardon you again this time," said the Fairy, "but woe to you if you play any more of your tricks on me."

Pinocchio gave a solemn oath that he would study and that he would always behave well, and he kept his word for the rest of the year. Indeed, at the exams he had the honour to be the cleverest boy in the school, and his behaviour earned praise and gave so much pleasure to everyone that the Fairy was completely satisfied and said to him,

"Tomorrow your wish shall finally come true!"

"What is that?"

"Tomorrow you will no longer be a puppet made of wood but will become a real boy."

Anyone who did not see the joy of Pinocchio at this news which he had been longing for, simply could not imagine it. All his friends and schoolmates had to be invited the following day to a great party in the Fairy's house to celebrate the great event. The Fairy promised to prepare two hundred chocolate drinks and four hundred scones buttered on both sides. That day promised to be so beautiful and so full of happiness but. . . .

It is unfortunate that in the life of a puppet there is always a "but" which spoils everything.

CHAPTER 30

Instead of becoming a boy, Pinocchio leaves home secretly with his friend, Lucignolo,* for the land of Fun-and-Games.

Pinocchio immediately asked the Fairy for permission to go around the town and make the invitations, and the Fairy said,

"You may go and invite your schoolmates to the party tomorrow, but remember to return home before night time. Do you understand?"

"I promise to be back within an hour."

"Be careful now, Pinocchio! Boys are quick to make promises, but more often than not they are slow to keep them."

"But I am not like the others. When I say a thing, I keep to it."

"We shall see. If you disobey it will be a sorry day."

"Why?"

"Because boys who do not listen to the advice of those who know better than they do, always get into trouble."

"I've certainly proved it!" said Pinocchio. "But I'll never make the same mistake again."

"We'll see if you speak the truth."

Without adding another word, the puppet kissed the good Fairy, who was to him a mother, and went out of the door singing and dancing.

*In Italian, Lucignolo is pronounced "Loo-cheen-yo-lo" and means "Candlewick."

In a little more than an hour, all his friends had been invited. Some accepted at once very gladly; others were a little slow to accept at first, but when they knew that the scones for dipping in the chocolate drink would be buttered on both sides, they all finished up by saying, "We shall come too, to make you happy."

Now I must tell you that among his friends and schoolmates there was one whom Pinocchio liked most of all. His name was Romeo, but everyone called him by the nickname of Lucignolo because he had such a lean and wiry body that it looked just like the wick of a new candle. Lucignolo was the laziest and naughtiest boy in the whole school but Pinocchio liked him very much. He went to search for him at home to invite him to the party, but could not find him there. He returned a second time and Lucignolo was still not home. He returned a third time, and searched the street in vain. Wherever would he find him? He searched for him everywhere, and finally found him hidden under the veranda of a farmer's house.

"What are you doing there?" asked the puppet.

"I'm waiting for midnight. I'm going away. . . ."

"Where are you going?"

"A long, long way away!"

"I've been to your home three times to look for you."

"What did you want me for?"

"Haven't you heard the big news? Don't you know the marvellous thing that has happened to me?"

"What is that?"

"Tomorrow I finish being a puppet and become a boy."

"A lot of good that will do you!"

"Tomorrow there's going to be a party at my place."

"But I told you that I'm leaving this evening."

"When?"

"At midnight."

"And where are you going?"

"I'm going to live in a town which is the most beautiful town in this world, a wonderful place!"

121

"And what is it called?"

"It's called the land of Fun-and-Games. Why don't you come too?"

"Me? Oh no!"

"You're wrong, Pinocchio. Believe me, if you don't come, you'll regret it. Where will you find a country more healthy for us boys? There's no school, no teachers, and no books. In this wonderful country you never have to study. You don't go to school on Thursday and every week is made up of six Thursdays and a Sunday. Just imagine! School holidays begin on the first day of January and end on the last day of December. It's a country that is just the place for me! That's how all civilized countries should be!"

"But how do you pass the time in the land of Fun-and-Games?"

"You pass the time by playing and amusing yourself from morning to night. At night you go to bed and in the morning it begins all over again. Does it appeal to you?"

"Umm . . . !" said Pinocchio and moved his head slowly from side to side as if to say, "It's a life that I would gladly live."

"You'll come with me then? Yes or no? Make up your mind."

"No, no, no, and no again. I have now promised to my good Fairy to become a real boy and I intend to keep the promise. I notice that the sun has nearly gone down, so I must leave you at once and get along. Goodbye, and safe journey."

"Where are you running to in such a hurry?"

"Home. The good Fairy wants me to return before night."

"Wait another two minutes."

"It will make me too late."

"Only two minutes."

"And what will the Fairy say to me then?"

"Let her say it. When she's had her say, she'll keep quiet," said that rascal of a Lucignolo.

"How are you going to travel? Will you be alone or with others?"

"Alone? There will be more than a hundred boys."

"And do you make the journey on foot?"

"At midnight a coach will pass by here which will take us to this wonderful country."

"I only wish it were midnight now!" said Pinocchio.

"Why?"

"So that I could see you all leave together."

"Just stay here a little longer, and you'll see us."

"No, no. I must go home."

"Wait another two minutes."

"I have delayed too long already. The Fairy will be worried about me."

"Poor Fairy! Is she afraid perhaps that the bats will eat you?"

"Look here," added Pinocchio, "are you absolutely sure that in this country there is no school at all?"

"Not a shadow of it."

"And no teachers?"

"Not a single one."

"And there is no need to study?"

"Never, never, never!"

"What a marvellous country," said Pinocchio, feeling his mouth beginning to water.

"Why don't you come too?"

"It's useless for you to tempt me! I have promised my good Fairy that I'll become a boy with good sense and I don't want to break my word."

"Then goodbye, and give my best wishes to all the high schools and grammar schools as you pass them along the way."

"Goodbye, Lucignolo, have a good trip, enjoy yourself, and think sometimes of your friends."

Having said that the puppet took two paces, but then, stopping and turning to his friend, he said,

"Are you absolutely sure that in this country the weeks are all made up of Thursdays and a Sunday?"

123

"Absolutely sure."

"And you know for certain that the school holidays begin on the first of January and finish on the last day of December?"

"For a certainty!"

"What a wonderful country!" repeated Pinocchio who had to spit because his mouth was watering so much.

Then, having made a firm resolution, he added quickly, "Well, goodbye once and for all, and safe journey."

"Goodbye."

"About what time will you leave?"

"In about two hours!"

"What a pity! If it were only an hour until you left I could almost wait."

"And the Fairy . . .?"

"I've left it too late already! . . . It makes no difference whether I return home one hour late or two hours late."

"Poor Pinocchio! And if the Fairy scolds you?"

"Too bad! Let her scold. When she has had her say, she'll be quiet."

Meanwhile it was already night, and the sky was very dark. Quite suddenly they saw moving in the distance a very small light and they heard the sound of donkey bells and a little squeal of trumpets, so small and faint that they seemed like the hum of a mosquito.

"Here it is!" cried Lucignolo, jumping to his feet.

"What is it?" asked Pinocchio in a low voice.

"It's the coach that is coming to take me. Well, do you want to come, yes or no?"

"But is it really true," asked the puppet, "that in this country the boys do not need to study?"

"Never, never, never!"

"What a wonderful country! . . . What a wonderful country! . . . What a wonderful country! . . ."

CHAPTER 31

Pinocchio reaches the land of Fun-and-Games and enjoys himself for five months. Then one morning he receives an unpleasant surprise.

At length the coach arrived, and it did not make any noise at all because the wheels were wrapped with straw and cloth. It was drawn by twelve pairs of donkeys, all the same size, but with different coloured coats—some were grey, some white, some sprinkled with white and grey like salt and pepper, and others had black and yellow stripes.

But the most unusual thing was this: those twenty-four donkeys, instead of being shod with iron shoes as are other beasts that drew carts, were wearing men's boots of white cow hide.

And what about the driver of the coach?

Just imagine to yourself a little man broader than he was long, all smooth and soft like a ball of butter, with a round little face, a little mouth that was always laughing, and a quiet, caressing voice, just like the purring of a cat when it's stroked.

All the boys liked him as soon as they saw him, and jostled with one another to get into the coach, to be led by him into that paradise known on the maps by the enticing name of land of Fun-and-Games. The carriage was already quite full of little boys between eight and twelve years, all heaped one on the other, like so many sardines in a tin.

They were uncomfortable, they were crushed, they

could hardly breathe, but no one cried and no one complained. The consolation of knowing that in a few hours they would arrive in a country where there were no books, no schools, and no teachers, made them so happy that they did not even notice if they were uncomfortable, tired, or hungry.

The coach had hardly come to a halt before the little man turned to Lucignolo and, with much smiling and rubbing of the hands, said to him laughingly,

"Tell me, my dear little boy, do you want to come to this wonderful country?"

"Oh, yes, I'm certain that I want to come."

"But I must warn you, my little dear, that there is no more room in the coach. As you see, it is quite full."

"Never mind," replied Lucignolo, "if there is not room inside I shall be happy to sit on the shafts of the coach." And taking a leap he landed astride the shafts.

"And you, my love?" said the little man turning very obligingly to Pinocchio. "What would you like to do? Will you come with us, or stay?"

"I'm staying," answered Pinocchio. "I want to study and do well at school, as all the other real boys do."

"A lot of good that will do you!"

"Pinocchio," said Lucignolo. "Please take my advice. Come with us and we'll be happy."

"No, no, no!"

"Come with us and we'll be happy," cried a few voices from within the carriage.

"Come with us and we'll be happy!" repeated a hundred voices from within the carriage.

"And if I come with you, what will my good Fairy say?" asked the puppet who was beginning to weaken.

"Don't worry your head with such gloomy thoughts. Just think that we're going into a country where we'll be able to make all the noise we want to from morning to night."

Pinocchio did not answer. He sighed once, twice, three times. Finally he said,

"Make a little room for me. I'm coming too! . . ."

"The places are all full," said the little man "but to show you how welcome you are I shall give you my place on the driver's seat."

"And you?"

"I'll walk along the road on foot."

"No, I couldn't allow that. I would rather get on to the back of one of these donkeys."

This was no sooner said than done. He went up to the right hand donkey in the first pair and moved as if he were going to get on its back, but the little beast, turning around, butted him heavily in the stomach so that he landed with his feet in the air.

You can easily imagine the burst of loud, rude laughter from all those boys who saw this, but the little man did not laugh. Full of loving kindness, he went up to the rebellious donkey and, pretending to give him a kiss, he took off in one bite half of his left ear.

Meanwhile Pinocchio was sitting on the ground and was very much annoyed. He stood up and jumped onto the back of that poor animal. The jump was such a good one that the boys stopped laughing and began to call out, "Good on you, Pinocchio!" and to applaud him loudly for a long time. Then suddenly the donkey lifted his two hind legs and bucked so violently that he threw the poor puppet into the middle of the road on top of a pile of stones. The loud laughing started again, but the little man, instead of laughing, showed his love for the restless little donkey by giving him a kiss that took clear away half of the other ear. Then he said to the puppet,

"Get on his back again and don't be afraid. That donkey has taken it into his head to play up, but I have had a few little words in his ears and I think that he will now be more tame and reasonable."

Pinocchio climbed on the animal's back and the coach began to move. But while the donkeys were trotting along and the carriage was rolling along the main road, the puppet seemed to catch the sound of a little voice, very soft and hard to hear, which said,

"Poor fool! You wanted your own way but you will repent it."

Pinocchio, very afraid, looked around to find out where these words came from, but he saw no one. The donkeys trotted and the carriage moved along. The boys inside were all asleep, Lucignolo snored like a bull-frog, and the little man seated outside sung between his teeth,

"All night they sleep
But I sleep never"

After another mile, Pinocchio heard the same little voice that said to him,

"Remember this, you little fool! The boys that give up studying and turn their backs on books and school and teachers, just for the sake of playing games and amusing themselves, always come to an unfortunate end! I have proved it, so I can tell you! One day you, too, will weep, as I weep today . . . But then it will be too late!"

At these words, whispered quietly, the puppet became more afraid than ever. He jumped down from the back of the donkey and went and held it by the nose.

How surprised he was when he saw that the donkey was weeping tears, just like a little boy.

"Oh I say, sir," called out Pinocchio to the driver of the coach. "Do you know what's happened now? This donkey is crying."

"Let it cry; it will laugh when it's married."

"Did you teach it to speak, by any chance?"

"No, it has taught itself to mumble a few words. It lived for three years in the company of trained dogs."

"Poor beast!"

"Move away there, move away!" said the little man. "Let us not lose our time by looking at a crying donkey. Get up again and let's go. The night is cool and the road is long."

Pinocchio obeyed without delay; the coach got under way again and in the morning, at dawn, they arrived happily in the land of Fun-and-Games.

The town they stopped at was not like any other in the world. The whole population was made up of boys. The oldest were fourteen years old, the youngest hardly eight. In the streets there was laughter and shouting, enough to lift your head off! Groups of little lads were gathered everywhere. Some were playing knucklebone, others threw balls, others rode on bikes, some were on wooden horses, others played blind-man's-buff. Some played hide-and-seek, while others who were dressed like clowns pretended to eat lighted straw. Some children were reciting, some were singing, others were doing somersaults, some were amusing themselves by walking on their hands with their legs in the air, others were rolling hoops, others were dressed like a general with a helmet of paper and were playing with cardboard soldiers. Some were laughing, some were shouting, others were calling out, some clapped their hands, others whistled, others imitated the noise of a hen laying an egg. There was such a pandemonium, so much talking and such a loud din that it was necessary to put cotton wool in your ears so as not to go deaf. In all the streets there were little theatres crowded with boys from morning to night, and on the walls of the houses such clever things as this had been written: "Long live gayms"; "No more skool"; "Down with rithmatik," and others of that kind.

Pinocchio, Lucignolo, and all the other boys who had made the trip with the little man, had hardly put their feet on the ground when they were immediately caught up in the midst of the hubbub, and within a few minutes they were friends with everyone.

Who could have been more happier and pleased than they were? The hours, the days, and the weeks passed in a twinkling while they played games and amused themselves.

"Oh what a wonderful life!" said Pinocchio every time that he happened to run into Lucignolo.

"You can see then that I was right?" Lucignolo asked. "And just to think that you did not want to leave home! And to think that you nearly returned to the Fairy's place to waste your time studying. . . . Today you are free from the bother of books and school and you owe it to me. It all came about because you took my advice. Isn't that so? It's only a true friend who does you that kind of favour."

"It's true, Lucignolo! But for you I would not be such a happy boy today. And just to think what that teacher said to me about you! He always said to me, "Have nothing to do with that rascal of a Lucignolo, because Lucignolo is a bad lad and the only advice he could give you is bad advice!""

"That poor old teacher!" answered the other, shaking his head. "I know he did not like me, and always amused himself by finding fault with me, but I am generous and I forgive him!"

"What a good fellow you are!" said Pinocchio embracing his friend affectionately and giving him a kiss on the cheek.

Five months had already gone by in that paradise where they played and amused themselves the whole day without ever having to see a book or a school, when one day Pinocchio, on waking up, received a most unpleasant surprise that put him in a very bad humour.

CHAPTER 32

Pinocchio grows ears like a donkey, and then he becomes a real donkey and begins to bray.

And what surprise was this? I shall tell you, my dear little readers. The surprise was that Pinocchio, on waking, scratched his head out of habit, and in scratching his head he noticed. . . . Do you think you can guess what he noticed?

He noticed to his very great surprise that his ears had grown more than six inches.

You will remember that the puppet had had very tiny ears since he was born. You could hardly see them with your bare eyes. Just imagine then how he felt when he became aware that his ears during the night had become so large that they were like two brooms.

He went in search of a mirror at once so that he could see himself. But as he could not find one he filled the washbasin with water and looked at his reflection in the water. He would sooner not have seen what he did. His face was decorated with a magnificent pair of donkey's ears!

I leave it to you to think how much sorrow and shame poor Pinocchio felt!

He began to cry and to scream and to hit his head against the wall, but the more he made these desperate noises the more his ears grew and grew and became hairy towards the top.

At the sound of these sharp cries, a beautiful little

squirrel entered the room. She lived on the floor above. When she saw the puppet in such a state she asked him timidly,

"What's the matter, my dear little neighbour?"

"I am sick, my little squirrel. I am very sick. I have a fever that makes me very much afraid. Do you know how to take a person's pulse?"

"I think so."

"Do you know then if by any chance I have a fever?"

The little squirrel lifted her right paw up and after having taken Pinocchio's pulse she said to him with a sigh,

"My friend, I am sorry that I have some bad news for you."

"What is it?"

"You have a very nasty fever."

"And what is the fever called?"

"It is donkey fever."

"I don't know this fever!" replied the puppet, who had understood only too well.

"Then I shall explain it to you," said the squirrel. "I must tell you that within two or three hours you will no longer be a puppet, or a boy. . . ."

"What shall I be?"

"Within two or three hours you will become a donkey, just like those that draw little carts which carry cabbages and lettuces to market."

"Oh no, oh no!" cried Pinocchio, grabbing with his hands at those two ears and pulling and tugging them fiercely as if they had been someone else's.

"My dear," said the squirrel to make him calm down. "What good will that do? It will not stop what is going to happen. It is a true and wise saying that all those who grow tired of books, schools, and teachers, and pass their days in games and amusements, will finish up sooner or later by changing into little donkeys."

"But is this really so?" asked the puppet sobbing.

133

"I am afraid it is, and crying is useless. You should have taken thought before!"

"But it's not my fault. Believe me, my dear squirrel, it's all Lucignolo's fault!"

"And who is this Lucignolo?"

"A schoolmate of mine. I wanted to return home; I wanted to be obedient; I wanted to continue studying and make others proud of me. . . . But Lucignolo said to me 'Why do you want to bother yourself with studying? Why do you want to go to school? Instead of that you should come with me to the land of Fun-and-Games. There we shall not study any more; there we shall amuse ourselves from morning to night and always be happy'."

"And why did you follow the advice of this false friend, of this bad companion?"

"Why? Because, my dear little squirrel, I am a puppet without sense and without heart. . . . Oh! If I had the least bit of a heart in me I would not have left the good Fairy who loved me just like a mother and who had done so much for me! And at this moment I would no longer be a puppet. . . . Instead I'd be a sensible boy just like all the others! Oh! If I meet Lucignolo, he had better watch out! I'll give him something that he won't forget in a hurry!" And he made as if to go out. But when he was at the door he remembered that he had donkey's ears, and because he was too ashamed to show himself in public, what do you think he did? He put a cotton cap on his head and pulled it right down over his ears.

Then he went out and began to search everywhere for Lucignolo. He searched in the streets, in the squares, in the little theatres, everywhere, but did not find him. He asked everyone he met along the way if they had seen him, but no one had.

Then he went to look for him at home. He reached his door and knocked.

"Who is it?" asked Lucignolo from within.

"It's me," answered the puppet.

"Just wait a moment and I'll let you in."

After half an hour the door opened. You can imagine how Pinocchio stared when he entered the house and saw his friend Lucignolo with a large cotton cap on his head, almost reaching down to his nose.

At the sight of this cap Pinocchio felt a little better, and said to himself quickly,

"Can it be that my friend has the same sickness as myself? Can it be that he has the donkey fever too?"

He pretended to notice nothing and asked laughingly, "How are you, my dear Lucignolo?"

"Very well. Just like a mouse in a block of cheese."

"Do you really mean that?"

"Why should I tell you a lie?"

"Excuse me, my friend, but why are you wearing that cotton cap that covers all your ears?"

"The doctor has ordered it for me because I have some pain in this knee. And you, my dear puppet, why are you wearing that cap pulled right down on your head?"

"The doctor ordered it for me because I have knocked some skin off my foot."

"Oh, my poor Pinocchio!"

"Oh, my poor Lucignolo!"

At these words there was a very long silence during which the two friends did nothing except look at one another as if they were making fun of each other.

At length the puppet said to his friend in an innocent little voice,

"Satisfy my curiosity, my dear Lucignolo? Have you ever suffered a sickness of the ears?"

"Never! And you?"

"Never! However, since this morning I have had some pain in one ear."

"I have the same pain."

"You too? Which ear is hurting?"

"Both. And you?"

"Both also."

"Perhaps it is the same illness."

"I am afraid it is. Would you do me a favour, Lucignolo?"

"With all my heart."

"Would you let me see your ears?"

"Why not? But first I would like to see yours, my dear Pinocchio."

"No. I should see yours first."

"No, my dear fellow. First you and then me!"

"Well," the puppet said, "Let us come to an agreement like good friends."

"What do you mean?"

"We shall each lift our cap at the same time. Do you agree?"

"I agree."

"Ready?" said Pinocchio, and he began to count in a loud voice, "One, two, three!"

At the word "three" the two boys pulled their caps from their heads and threw them in the air. And then there was a scene that would have been incredible if it were not true. When Pinocchio and Lucignolo saw that they had both suffered the same misfortune they were not nearly so unhappy. They began to twitch their enormous ears, and after making many rude little signs finished up by breaking into loud laughter. They laughed and laughed and laughed so much that they had to hold their sides in. Then in the middle of a big burst of laughter Lucignolo all of a sudden fell quiet and started to stagger about and change colour.

"Help, help, Pinocchio!" he called to his friend.

"What's the matter?"

"Ohh! I can't manage to stand straight on my feet."

"Nor can I!" cried Pinocchio, crying and swaying about.

And while they said this they both bent down on their hands and knees on the ground and began walking about on all fours. They they started running around the room, and while they were running their hands and feet changed into hoofs and their faces grew longer and became donkeys' muzzles and their backs were covered with light grey fur speckled with black.

But the worst moment for those two miserable boys was still to come. Do you know what it was?

The worst and most humiliating moment was when they felt themselves sprouting tails from behind. Overcome with shame and grief, they began to cry and feel sorry for themselves.

They wished they had not been so thoughtless and lazy! Instead of sobs and cries, the braying of asses came out of their mouths. They brayed loudly in chorus,

"Hee-haw, hee-haw, hee-haw."

Just then there was a knock at the door and a voice from outside said,

"Open the door! It's the little man, the driver of the coach that brought you into this country. Open the door at once or you'll be sorry!"

CHAPTER 33

Pinocchio becomes a real donkey and is taken to be sold. He is bought by the ringmaster of a circus who intends to teach him to dance and to jump through hoops; but one evening he lames himself and is then sold to a man who wants to use his skin for a drum.

When the door was not opened the little man forced it wide open with a violent kick. He came into the room and said in his usual laughing little voice to Pinocchio and Lucignolo,

"Clever boys! You brayed well and I recognized you at once by your voices. That's why I'm here."

At these words the two donkeys were very quiet and stood with their heads down, their ears low, and their tails between their legs. At first the little man stroked them, caressed them, and patted them. Then he pulled out a comb and began to comb them vigorously. When their coats were shining like two mirrors he put halters on them and led them to the market square. He hoped to sell them and make a little profit.

He did not have to wait long for buyers. Lucignolo was bought by a farmer whose donkey had died the day before, and Pinocchio was sold to the ringmaster of a circus, who bought him to teach him how to dance and jump through hoops with the other animals of the company.

By now, my little readers, you will have realized what a fine trade that little man carried on. The nasty little brute, who had a face like milk and honey, went from place to place with his cart, day after day, all over the world. On the way he collected, by means of promises and coaxing, all the lazy boys who had grown sick of books and school.

When he had loaded them into his cart he led them to the land of Fun-and-Games where they passed all their time in games, noise, and fun. After a time these poor, silly little boys, through playing all the time and never studying, changed into donkeys. The little man, pleased with this change, made himself master of them and took them to be sold at fairs and markets. And so in a few years he had become a millionaire.

I do not know what happened to Lucignolo, but I know that Pinocchio, from the very start, led a very hard life.

When he was taken into his stall the ringmaster filled the manger with straw. Pinocchio tried a mouthful and spat it out. The ringmaster grumbled and filled the manger with hay, but even that did not please Pinocchio.

"Ahh! So the hay doesn't please you either," cried the ringmaster, becoming annoyed. "We'll see about that, my pretty little donkey. If you've got some fancy ideas, I'll cure you of those!" And by way of correction he gave him a good whipping on the legs.

Pinocchio began to weep and bray, and while he brayed he said,

"Hee-haw, hee-haw. I can't digest straw."

"Then eat the hay!" replied the ringmaster, who understood very well the dialect of donkeys.

"Hee-haw, hee-haw, The hay makes me sick!"

"Do you suggest that a mule, like you, should be fed on breast of chicken and leg of pork?" replied the ringmaster, becoming angrier still and giving him a second whipping on the legs.

At that second whipping, Pinocchio became quiet and said no more. The stall door was shut and Pinocchio was left alone. Because it was many hours since he had eaten, he began to suffer from a gnawing hunger; his stomach felt terribly empty, just like a big oven.

At length, finding nothing else in the manger, he resigned himself to chewing a little hay. When he had chewed it very well he shut his eyes, gulped, and swallowed it.

"This hay isn't too bad," he said to himself, "but how much better it would have been if I'd kept on studying. At this moment I would have been enjoying a snack of fresh bread with slices of pork sausage, not this hay! But it's no use complaining now!"

Next morning, on waking up, he searched in the manger for a little hay but did not find any because he had eaten it all in the night. He took a mouthful of cut straw but while he was chewing it he couldn't help noticing that the smell of the cut straw was not at all like the smell of a plateful of rice and meat, or macaroni and cheese.

"It's no use complaining!" he repeated to himself and kept on chewing. "At least my misfortune should serve as a lesson to all the disobedient boys who do not want to study. It's too bad! Just too bad!"

"Too bad, the devil!" shouted the ringmaster coming into the stall at that moment. "Do you believe perhaps, my dear little donkey, that I have bought you just for the sake of giving you food and drink? I bought you so that you can work; you will have to earn me some money. Up now, my clever one! Come with me to the circus ring and there I shall teach you to jump through hoops, to break the paper of the hoop with your head, and to dance the waltz and the polka standing upright on your back legs."

Poor Pinocchio had to learn all these wonderful things whether he liked it or not, but the learning of them required three months of lessons and many whippings that made him sore.

Finally the day came when the ringmaster was able to announce a truly extraordinary spectacle. The posters of many colours, placed at the street corners, read as follows:

GALA PERFORMANCE
This evening's entertainment will include
HIGH JUMPS AND REMARKABLE FEATS OF ACROBATICS
followed by many other acts with artists and horses
and presenting for the first time the famous
PINOCCHIO THE DONKEY
known as
THE STAR OF THE DANCE
* * * * *
The theatre will be completely illuminated

That evening, as you can imagine, the theatre was
crowded out an hour before the spectacle was due to
commence. It was not possible to find a seat, not even
a reserved place or a box, and you could not have
bought one for gold.

The seats in the circus were overflowing with very
young children and boys and girls of all ages who were
waiting, full of excitement, to see the dancing of the
famous donkey, Pinocchio.

When the first part of the show was over, the ringmaster, dressed in a black coat, white breeches, and
shiny leather boots that came right up to his knees,
presented himself before the huge crowd of people
and made a deep bow.

He delivered this speech with great solemnity:
"Ladies and gentlemen!

"My journeys have brought me to your famous city
where it is my great honour, as well as my sincere
pleasure, to present to this intelligent and worthy
audience a famous donkey which has already had the
honour of dancing before the kings and queens of all
the largest countries in Europe.

"Thank you for your attendance, one and all! With
your encouragement, and your kindness, we shall now
commence!"

This speech was greeted with much laughter and
much applause, but the applause grew louder and

became a kind of hurricane at the appearance of the donkey, Pinocchio, in the middle of the circus arena.

He was all decked out for the occasion. He had a new bridle of shiny leather with buckles and fittings of brass, two white camellias at his ears, his mane laid out in a great number of curls bound with tassels of red silk, a gold and silver cover fixed down the middle of his back, and his tail was plaited with ribbons of blue and purple velvet. He was a donkey for everyone to love.

The ringmaster presented him to the public with these words:

"Most respected audience!

"I shall not delay proceedings at this stage by mentioning the very difficult task undertaken by me in capturing and taming this mammal, while it was grazing in its natural state on the mountains in the hottest part of the world. Observe, I beg you, how much of the wild animal still glows in those eyes because, having tried in vain all known methods of training him to the life of a domesticated animal, I was often obliged to use the friendly language of the whip. But every kindness of mine, instead of making him love me, has for the most part, only succeeded in forcing him to obey me.

"I have, however, followed the system of Colles, and have found in his skull a small bony area that the Doctors of Medicine in Paris recognize as the part of the body that makes hair grow and makes dancing possible. By means of this I willed him to master not only dancing, but the art of jumping and of leaping through hoops covered with paper. See him and judge for yourself! Before that, however, permit me, kind sirs, permit me to invite you to the performance tomorrow evening. And in the event of storm clouds threatening rain, the performance will be postponed to the following day, at eleven o'clock, one hour before noon."

The ringmaster bowed deeply. Then, turning to Pinocchio, he said:

"Step forward, Pinocchio! Before commencing your exercises, greet this notable audience of ladies, gentlemen, and children."

Pinocchio, now obedient, knelt down quickly on his two front knees almost to the ground and remained in that position until the moment when the ringmaster, cracking his whip, cried out to him, "Walk!"

Then the donkey stood up and commenced to move around the arena, all the time keeping to a walk.

After a few minutes the ringmaster cried,

"At the trot!"

And Pinocchio, obedient to orders, changed his pace to a trot.

"At the gallop!"

And Pinocchio broke into a gallop.

"At full speed!"

And Pinocchio began to run at full speed.

But while he was running like a racehorse, the ringmaster lifted his arm in the air and fired a shot from a pistol. At the sound of that shot, Pinocchio fell down onto the floor of the arena and lay there as if he were dead.

When he rose from the ground there was a great burst of applause, shouts, and hand-clapping. He lifted his head to receive the applause and saw . . . and saw . . . in one of the boxes, a beautiful lady who had around her neck a large gold chain from which hung a locket. In the locket there was a painting of a puppet.

"That's a painting of me! That lady is the Fairy!" Pinocchio said to himself, recognizing her at once. He was overcome with happiness and tried to cry—"Oh, my dear Fairy! Oh, my dear Fairy!"

But instead of these words there came out of his throat a bray so loud and prolonged that it made all the spectators laugh, and especially all the boys in the circus.

Then the ringmaster, in order to teach him obedience and to make him understand that it was not good manners to bray in public, gave him a smack on the nose with his whip.

The poor donkey stuck out his six inches of tongue and licked his nose for at least five minutes, perhaps hoping in that way to wash away all the sadness that he felt.

You can imagine how great a feeling of despair came over him when he turned to look at the box a second time and saw that it was empty and that the Fairy had disappeared.

He thought he must surely die. His eyes filled with tears and he began to cry. No one, however, was aware of this, not even the ringmaster, who cracked his whip and shouted, "Ready now, Pinocchio! You are going to show these people how gracefully you can jump through hoops."

Pinocchio tried two or three times, but each time when he arrived at the hoop he found it easier to pass beneath instead of jumping through it. Finally he took off and jumped through but unluckily his back legs caught on the hoop, with the result that he fell heavily to the ground on the other side.

When he stood up he discovered that he had made himself lame and only with difficulty was he able to return to his stable.

"Bring back Pinocchio! We want Pinocchio! Bring back Pinocchio!" cried the children in the theatre who were all very sorry because of the accident.

But the donkey was not seen again that evening.

Next morning the animal doctor was called to visit him and announced that he would remain lame for the rest of his life.

Then the ringmaster said to the stable boy,

"What do you expect me to do with a lame donkey? He will be nothing but a useless loafer. Take him to the market place and sell him."

When they reached the market place they found at once a buyer who asked the stable boy, "How much do you want for this lame donkey?"

"Five dollars."

"I will give you five dollars. Don't think that I'm buying him to serve me—I'm buying him only for his skin. I see that he has a very hard skin, and that is just what I want to make a drum for the band in my village."

What a shock and surprise it was to poor Pinocchio to hear that he was to become a drum!

The buyer paid the five dollars and led the donkey to some rocks on the seashore. He put a stone around Pinocchio's neck for a weight, and tied a rope to one leg. He held the other end of the rope in his hand and gave the donkey a shove which sent him into the water.

Pinocchio, with the stone around his neck, went straight to the bottom. The buyer held the rope in his hand and sat down on the rock to wait while the donkey drowned so that he could take off his skin.

CHAPTER 34

Pinocchio, having been thrown into the sea, is eaten by the fish and becomes a puppet again. While he is swimming to save himself he is swallowed by the terrible Sea Monster.

After the donkey had been under the water for fifteen minutes the buyer said to himself,

"By this time the poor lame donkey should be well and truly drowned. I'll pull him up now and use his skin to make a drum."

He began to draw on the rope which he had tied round one of the legs. He pulled and pulled until he saw, coming out of the water . . . Can you guess?

Instead of a dead donkey he saw coming out of the water a live puppet who was wriggling like an eel. When he saw the wooden puppet the poor man thought he must be dreaming. He stood there bewildered, his mouth open, and his eyes standing out of his head.

When he had collected himself a little he managed to say,

"Where's the donkey that I threw into the sea?"

"I'm that donkey," answered the puppet laughing.

"You?"

"Me."

"Oh, you rogue! I think you're trying to make a fool of me."

"Make a fool of you? That is not true, my dear sir. I'm quite serious."

"But you were a donkey a short time ago. How can you come out of the water as a wooden puppet?"

"It must be the effect of salt water. The sea plays these tricks."

"Watch out, puppet! Watch out! Don't try to amuse yourself at my expense. You'll be sorry if I lose my patience."

"Well then, my good sir, would you like to know the true story? Release this leg of mine and I'll tell it to you."

The curious buyer, eager to know the full story, quickly untied the knot in the rope. Then Pinocchio, finding himself free as a bird, said to him,

"Once I was a wooden puppet just as I am today. I was about to become a real boy, just like all the others in this world, and I would have done so but for my laziness about studying and my habit of listening to bad companions. I ran away from home. . . . And one fine day I woke up to find myself changed into a donkey with long ears. . . . And what a tail! . . . It was a great shame for me . . . a shame that the Holy St. Anthony would not make even you experience! I was taken to the market of the asses where I was bought by the ringmaster of a circus. He wanted to make me into a great dancer, and taught me to jump through hoops. But one evening, during the show, I had a bad fall in the arena and was left lame in two legs. Then the ringmaster, not knowing what to do with a lame donkey, sent me to be sold again, and you bought me."

"And what bad luck for me! I paid five dollars, and who will give me back my five dollars now?"

"But just think why you bought me! You bought me to make my skin into a drum . . . a drum!"

"What bad luck for me! Where shall I find another skin?"

"Don't give up hope; there are lots of donkeys in this world!"

"Well, my young rascal, is that the end of your story?"

"No; just a few more words and then it is finished.

147

You bought me and led me to this place to kill me, but then you gave in to your kinder feelings. You cared enough for me to tie a stone around my neck and throw me to the bottom of the sea. This kindly feeling does you great honour and I shall always remember you for it. However, dear sir, you made your plans without taking into account the Fairy. . . ."

"And who is this Fairy?"

"She is my mother, and she's just like all the other good mothers who love their children very much and never lose sight of them. They help them lovingly in every misfortune, even when those children, because they are thoughtless and naughty, do not deserve any help at all. When the good Fairy saw me in danger of drowning, she sent at once a huge shoal of fish. The fish thought I was a real donkey who was quite dead, and began to eat me! And what big mouthfuls they took! I would never had believed that fish had bigger appetites than boys. One ate my ears, one ate my nose, another the neck and the mane, another the skin and the hoofs, another my back, and among the others there was a fish who even ate my tail."

"From this day forward," said the buyer horrified, "I swear never again to eat the flesh of fish. I could not bear the thought of opening a mullet or a whiting and finding in its stomach the tail of a donkey!"

"I agree with you," laughed the puppet. "But to continue, when the fish had finished eating all of the donkey flesh that covered me from head to tail they arrived at the bones. . . . Or rather, they arrived at the wood, because as you see I am made of very hard wood. After a few bites those greedy fish realized that wood was not suitable meat for their teeth. This tough food made them sick and they swam off in all directions, without even turning to thank me. And now you have heard the full story of how you came to find a live puppet tied on the end of the rope instead of a dead donkey."

"A very funny story, I'm sure!" said the buyer angrily. "I know that I have spent five dollars to buy you and I want my money back. Do you know what I'll do? I'll take you to the market and sell you by weight as seasoned firewood."

"You may sell me again. I am happy enough about that," said the puppet, but as he said this he gave a great leap and landed in the water. He swam happily and drew away from the shore, crying out to the poor buyer,

"Goodbye, kind sir. If you need some skin for a drum, please think of me." And then he laughed and kept on swimming.

After a little while, he turned back again and called out more loudly,

"Goodbye, kind sir. If you ever need a little seasoned wood for lighting the stove, be sure to think of me."

It was not long at all before he was so far from the shore that he could barely be seen. All that showed on the surface of the sea was a small black shape that lifted its legs out of the water occasionally and made jumps and leaps like a dolphin in a good mood.

When Pinocchio had been swimming for some time he noticed in the middle of the sea a rock that looked like white marble. And on the top of the rock a beautiful little goat was bleating affectionately and making signs for him to come closer. There was something very unusual about that little goat. Her coat was not white or black or marked with spots, like other goats, but was raven-coloured, and of such a glowing shade that it reminded the puppet very much of the hair of the good Fairy.

I am sure you can imagine how the little heart of Pinocchio started to beat! He redoubled his efforts and swam quickly towards the white rock. He was already halfway there when all of a sudden the huge and horrible head of a fish, with its mouth wide open, came out of the sea towards him. Its three rows of

teeth would have been terrifying even in a painting. Do you know what this terrible fish was? It was the gigantic Sea Monster, referred to many times in this story. Because of his many savage attacks and his enormous hunger he was known as the killer of fish and fishermen.

Poor Pinocchio was terribly scared at the sight of the Monster. He tried to avoid it, to change direction, to flee from it. But that immense open mouth kept on coming towards him with the speed of an arrow.

"Hurry, Pinocchio, for heaven's sake," cried the beautiful little goat.

Pinocchio swam desperately with his arms and legs and feet.

"Hurry, Pinocchio, hurry! The Monster is catching you!"

Pinocchio, summoning up all his strength, swam faster than ever.

"Watch out, Pinocchio! The Monster is nearly on you! Here he is! Here he is! Hurry for heaven's sake or you are lost!"

Pinocchio swam faster still, on and on and on, as if he were a bullet from a gun. He was already close to the rock and the little goat was bending down towards the sea, holding out her foot to help him out of the water.

But it was too late! The Monster had caught up to him. The Monster took a breath and drank down the poor little puppet as if he had been the yolk of an egg. He swallowed him with such violence and so hungrily that Pinocchio, falling down into the body of the Sea Monster, landed so heavily that he was knocked out and lay dazed for a quarter of an hour.

When he woke up again he could not at first gather his thoughts to find out just what world he was in. All around him, on every side, there was nothing but darkness; it was absolutely pitch black; he seemed to be resting with his head stuck in an inkstand full of black ink. He listened and did not hear a noise, but from time to time he felt some great blasts of wind beating against his face.

At first he could not understand where this wind came from, but gradually he realized that it was coming from the lungs of the Monster. The Sea Monster suffered very badly from asthma, and whenever he breathed he blew like the north wind.

From the start Pinocchio did his best to find a little courage, but when everything told him that he was shut up in the body of the Sea Monster he began to cry and call out,

"Help! Help! Oh, won't someone save me?"

"Who do you expect to save you, you unlucky fellow?" said a voice in the dark, a hoarse, cracked voice that sounded like a guitar out of tune.

"Who's that speaking?" asked Pinocchio, feeling himself freeze with fear.

"It's only me! I'm a poor tuna fish, swallowed by the Sea Monster at the same time as you. And what kind of fish are you?"

"I'm not any kind of fish. I'm a puppet."

"If you're not a fish, how did you come to get swallowed by the Monster?"

"I didn't ask to be swallowed, he just swallowed me! Can you tell me what we are going to do here in the dark?"

"Resign ourselves and wait until the Sea Monster has digested both of us."

"But I don't want to be digested," said Pinocchio.

"Nor do I," answered the tuna "but I'm a philosopher, and I console myself by thinking that when one is born a tuna it is better to die under the water than to be cooked in oil!"

"Foolishness!" cried the puppet.

"That is my opinion," answered the tuna, "and opinions, as the tuna politicians say, ought to be respected!"

"That's all very well, I suppose, but I want to get away from here . . . I want to escape. . . ."

"Escape if you can."

"Is this Sea Monster very big?" asked the puppet.

"Imagine to yourself a body that is more than a mile long, without counting the tail."

While they were holding this conversation in the dark Pinocchio seemed to see far away in the distance a very faint light.

"What could that little light be away in the distance?" he asked.

"That will be some companion of our misfortune who is waiting like us for the moment when he is digested."

"I'm going to find him. Isn't it possible that it could be some old fish who is able to show us the way to escape?"

"I wish you luck with all my heart, my dear puppet."

"Goodbye, tuna."

"Goodbye, puppet, and good luck."

"Where shall we meet again?"

"Who knows? It is better not even to think of it."

*In the body of the Sea Monster
Pinocchio meets ... Who does
he meet? Read this chapter
and find out.*

Pinocchio said goodbye to his good friend the tuna
and began to move by feeling his way in the dark. He
walked slowly through the body of the Sea Monster,
placing one foot before the other and heading for that
tiny, faint light that he saw blinking away in the
distance.

His feet squelched in pools of thick, slippery liquid
which gave off such a strong smell of fried fish that he
thought he must be in the middle of Lent.

The more he went forward the clearer the distant
light became until, after walking for a long time, he
finally reached it. And when he did so. . . . What did he
find?

If you had a thousand guesses you would still be
wrong. He found a small table standing there, and on
it a lighted candle fixed in a bottle of green glass, and
seated at the table a very old man with white hair,
like snow or whipped cream. This man sat there
munching some small fish, still alive, which wriggled
so much that while he was eating them they even
escaped out of his mouth.

At the sight of the old man Pinocchio felt such surprise and happiness that he was delirious with joy.
He wanted to laugh, he wanted to cry, and he wanted
to say a thousand things. Instead he stammered and

tripped over his words and could not say anything at all. At length he managed to get out a cry of joy, and throwing wide his arms he jumped on the neck of that old man and shouted,

"Oh, my dear old father, at last I have found you! Now I will never leave you again. Never, never, never!"

"Then my eyes tell me the truth?" asked the old man, rubbing his eyes. "You really are my dear little Pinocchio?"

"Yes, yes I am! It's really me! And you have already pardoned me, haven't you? Oh, my dear father, how good you are. And to think that I, on the other hand. . . . Oh! But if you knew how many misfortunes have rained on my head and how many things have gone wrong for me! Just picture the day, when you, my poor, dear old father, sold your old coat and bought me the school reader and I ran off to see the puppets and the owner of the puppets wanted to put me on the fire so that he could cook his roast mutton, and he was the one who gave me the five gold coins to bring to you but I met the fox and the cat who led me to the Inn of the Red Lobster where they ate like wolves, and when I was left alone in the night I met the highwaymen who ran after me, with me in front and them behind, on and on and on, with me always in front and them behind, until they caught me and hung me to the branch of the Giant Oak Tree where the beautiful girl with the raven-coloured hair sent for me to be taken in a carriage, and the doctors, when they were called in, said at once 'If he is not dead, it is a sign that he is still alive' and then I told a lie, and my nose began to grow and it grew so much that I could not get out through the door of the room, as a result of which I went with the fox and the cat to bury the four gold coins because I had spent one at the inn, and the parrot began to laugh and instead of two thousand coins I found nothing, for which the judge, when he knew that I had been robbed, immediately had me put in prison in order to give satisfaction to the thieves, from where, when I came away, I saw a beautiful bunch of grapes in a field, and I was caught in a trap and the farmer with good reason put a dog collar on me and made me guard the chickens, but when he knew my innocence he let me go, and the snake with the smoking tail began to laugh and burst a vein in his chest, and so I returned to the house of the beautiful girl, who was dead, and the dove seeing me cry said to me, 'I have seen your father who was building a little boat to go in search of you', and I said to him, 'Oh, if only I had wings,' and he said to me, 'Do you want to go to your father?' and I said to him 'Of course, but who can carry me?' and he said to me, 'I shall carry you there,' and I said 'How!' and he said to me 'Climb on my back!' and so we flew all the night and then in the morning the fishermen who were looking out to sea said to me, 'There is a poor man in a little boat who is going to sink,' and from the distance I recognized you at once because my heart told me it was you, and I made a sign to you to return to the shore. . . ."

"I recognized you also," said Geppetto. "I would gladly have returned to the shore but how was I to do it? The seas were very large and a great wave turned over the boat. The horrible Sea Monster who was near by had no sooner seen me in the water than he hurried over at once and put out his tongue and caught me in a moment and swallowed me like a meatball."

"And how long have you been shut up in here?" asked Pinocchio.

"From that day to this, which is now two years; two years my little Pinocchio, which have seemed two centuries."

"How have you managed to live? Where did you find the candle and the matches to light it? Who gave you those?"

"I shall tell you everything. First of all, the same storm that turned over my little boat also swamped a merchant ship. The sailors were all saved but the ship went to the bottom and the same Sea Monster, who that day had an excellent appetite, first swallowed me and then swallowed the whole ship. . . ."

"Do you mean to say that he swallowed it in a mouthful?" asked Pinocchio marvelling.

"In a mouthful, and he spat out only the main mast because it was stuck in his teeth like a scrap of food. By good luck, that ship was full of preserved meat in watertight boxes, biscuits, bread, bottles of wine, dry grapes, cheese, coffee, sugar, candlewax, and packets of wax matches. With all these good things from God I have been able to live for two years, but today I am at the last mouthful. Today there is nothing in the pantry, and this candle is the last one left. . . ."

"And after that?"

"And after that, my little dear, we two shall remain in the dark."

"In that case, my dear father," said Pinocchio, "we have no time to lose. We must discover at once how to escape."

"Escape? How?"

"By getting out through the mouth of the Sea Monster and throwing ourselves into the sea and swimming."

"That's easily said, my dear little Pinocchio, but I cannot swim."

"What does that matter? You will get on my back; I'm a very good swimmer, and will carry you safe and sound to the shore."

"I'm afraid you are imagining things, my dear boy," answered Geppetto shaking his head and smiling sadly. "Do you really think it is possible that a puppet, hardly three feet high, like yourself, would have the strength to carry me on his shoulders?"

"Let's try it and you'll see! And if it is meant that we should die, we shall at least have the great comfort of dying in one another's arms."

Without saying another word, Pinocchio took the candle in his hand and went forward to show the way. He said to his father,

"You follow behind me, and do not be afraid."

They walked a long way, passing right through the body and the stomach of the Sea Monster. When they reached the point where the great throat of the Monster began, they stopped to have a look around and to watch for the best moment to escape.

The Sea Monster was forced to sleep with his mouth open because he was very old and suffered from asthma and palpitations of the heart. Pinocchio approached the opening of the throat and by looking up it he was able to see, at the far end, the enormous open mouth and a large piece of the starlit sky and the beautiful light of the moon.

"This is the very moment to escape," he whispered as he turned to his father. "The Sea Monster is sleeping like a log. The sea is calm, and we can see just like daytime. Follow me, father dear, and we shall soon be saved."

They climbed up through the throat of the Sea Monster and reached his immense mouth. They began to walk on the tips of their toes along the tongue, a tongue so broad and long that it looked like a garden path. They were ready to make their big leap into the sea when all of a sudden the Sea Monster sneezed, and he shook so violently that Pinocchio and Geppetto found themselves thrown down and hurled once again into the bottom of the Sea Monster's stomach. While they tumbled over and over the candle went out, and they were left in the dark.

"What now?" asked Pinocchio, as he straightened himself up.

"Now, my boy, we are lost for good."

"Why lost? Give me your hand, daddy, and watch out you don't slip."

"Where are you taking me?"

158

"We are going back to try again. Come with me and don't be afraid."

Pinocchio took his father by the hand and they began walking on the tips of their toes and climbed together through the throat of the Monster. They crept along his tongue and climbed over the three rows of teeth. Before leaping into the sea the puppet said to his father,

"Climb on to my back, put your arms over my shoulders, and hold tight. Leave the rest to me."

Geppetto had no sooner placed himself firmly on the shoulders of his son than Pinocchio, full of confidence, jumped into the water and began to swim. The sea was as smooth as oil; the moon shone brightly in all its glory and the Sea Monster continued to sleep so heavily that not even a cannon shot would have woken him.

CHAPTER 36

While Pinocchio was swimming strongly towards the shore he noticed that his father, who was holding onto his back and had his legs in the water, was shivering all the time as though he was suffering from a high fever.

Pinocchio did not know if the old man was shivering from cold or fear, but he thought it was probably fear, and said to cheer him up,

"Have courage, daddy, in a few minutes we shall reach the land and be safe."

"But where is the shore?" asked the old man, becoming more and more anxious and screwing up his eyes as a tailor does when he is threading a needle.

"I've looked everywhere but all that I can see is the sky and the sea."

"But I can see the shore," said the puppet. "I have eyes like a cat; I can see better in the night than in the day."

Poor Pinocchio pretended to be cheerful but he was really beginning to lose heart. He was weak and out of breath. He could not keep going much longer and the shore was a long way off. He swam as long as he had breath, then he turned his head towards Geppetto and said with difficulty,

"Help me, daddy, I'm dying!"

Both father and son were on the point of drowning when they heard a voice like a tuneless guitar which said, "Who's dying?"

"My father and I!"

"I recognize that voice. It's Pinocchio!"

"That's right. And who are you?"

"I'm the tuna, your prison mate in the body of the Sea Monster."

"How did you escape?"

"I followed your example. You showed me the way, and after you had gone, I escaped also."

"My dear tuna, you have come along at the right moment. I beg you, for the love that I bear to your children, the little tuna, help us or we are lost."

"Gladly and with all my heart. Both of you hold on to my tail and leave it to me to lead the way. In four minutes I shall have you at the shore."

As you can imagine, Geppetto and Pinocchio accepted the invitation at once, but instead of holding on to the tail they thought that it would be more comfortable to seat themselves right on the back of the tuna.

"Are we too heavy?" Pinocchio asked him.

"Heavy? No more than a shadow. It feels like two sea shells," replied the tuna.

When they reached the shore Pinocchio jumped to land first so he could help his father, then he turned to the tuna and said with a voice full of emotion,

"My friend, you have saved my father. I haven't enough words to thank you. Allow me at least to give you a kiss to show that I shall never forget you."

The tuna put his nose out of the water and Pinocchio, leaning down on his knees, placed a most affectionate kiss on his mouth. At this sign of true tenderness, the poor tuna, who was not accustomed to it, was completely overcome. He dived under the waves and disappeared because he would have been ashamed if Pinocchio had seen his tears.

Meanwhile, day had broken.

Pinocchio offered his arm to Geppetto who had hardly the strength to hold himself on his feet, and said to him,

"Lean on my arm, my dear daddy, and let us go. We shall walk as slowly as the ants and when we are tired we shall rest along the way."

"And where shall we go?" asked Geppetto.

"We'll look for a house or a cottage where some kind person will give us a mouthful of bread to eat, and a little straw for a bed."

They had not taken more than a hundred steps when they saw, seated on the edge of the road, two ugly creatures who were begging alms.

It was the cat and the fox, but they could not be recognized for what they had been before.

The cat who had pretended to be blind, was now really blind; and the old fox had grown mangy, with patches of bare skin showing, and no longer had even a tail. The sad old thief had finally become so poor and hungry that he was forced to sell even his beautiful tail. It was bought by a travelling merchant who used it as a fly swat.

"Oh Pinocchio," cried the fox in a whining voice, "will you give a little something to two poor creatures who are old and sick?"

"Old and sick," repeated the cat.

"Goodbye, you rogues," replied the puppet. "You have tricked me once, but you won't catch me again."

"Believe me, Pinocchio, that today we are truly poor and wretched!"

"Truly poor and wretched!" repeated the cat.

"If you are poor, you deserve it. Remember the proverb that says, 'Stolen money does not increase.' Goodbye, you rogues."

"Have pity on us!"

"Goodbye, you rogues! Remember the proverb that says 'The wheat of the devil makes only chaff'."

"Don't abandon us!"

". . . abandon us!" repeated the cat.

"Goodbye, you rogues! Remember the proverb that says, 'He who steals his neighbour's cloak, usually does without a coat'."

Pinocchio and Geppetto then continued slowly along the road, until they saw at the end of a path, in the middle of a field, a hut of straw with a tiled roof.

"There must be someone living in that hut," said Pinocchio. "Let's go and knock at the door."

So they went and knocked at the door.

"Who is it?" asked a small voice from inside.

"It's a poor old father and a poor son without bread or a roof over their heads," answered the puppet.

"Turn the key and the door will open by itself," said the same little voice.

Pinocchio turned the key and the door opened. He entered and looked around on all sides, but he did not see anyone.

"Where's the master of this cottage?" said Pinocchio with wonder.

"Here I am, up here!"

Father and son immediately turned and looked at the ceiling, and there they saw on a beam the Talking Cricket.

"Oh! It's my dear little cricket!" said Pinocchio, greeting him courteously.

"Now you call me your 'dear little cricket,' don't you? Do you remember when you threw a hammer at me to drive me out of your house?"

"You're right, little cricket! Drive me out also, throw a hammer at me, but have pity on my poor old father."

"I shall have pity on the father and also on the son, but I wanted to remind you how badly you behaved before, and to teach you that in this life you must show kindness to everyone, on all occasions, if you wish to have the same kindness shown to you in your day of need."

"You are right, little cricket, you are certainly right, and I won't forget the lesson you have given me. But tell us how you came to own this cottage?"

"This cottage was given to me yesterday as a gift by a gracious little goat who has a coat of the most beautiful raven colour."

"And where has the goat gone?" asked Pinocchio.

"I don't know."

"When will she return?"

"She will never return. Yesterday she left very sadly, and while she bleated she seemed to be saying, 'Poor Pinocchio, I will never see him again. . . . The Sea Monster has devoured him!'."

"Did she really say that? . . . Then it was her . . . it was her . . . it was my dear little Fairy!"

Pinocchio cried and sobbed and wept.

When he had had a good cry, he dried his eyes. Then he prepared a neat little bed of straw and helped old Geppetto to lie down.

He said to the Talking Cricket,

"Can you please tell me, little cricket, where I can find a glass of milk for my poor father?"

"Three fields away from here there is a farmer called Giangio* who keeps cows. He will be able to give you some milk."

Pinocchio went at a run to the house of the farmer Giangio. The farmer said to him:

"How much milk do you want?"

"Just a glassful."

"A glassful of milk costs five cents. Please give me the five cents."

"I haven't even one cent," said Pinocchio very sadly.

"That's bad luck, my little puppet," replied the farmer. "If you haven't even a cent, I haven't even a thimbleful of milk."

"I see!" said Pinocchio hopelessly, and turned to go

---

*Pronounced in Italian "Jan-Joe."

"Hold on a moment," said Giangio, "perhaps we can work it out between the two of us. Would you like to try turning the bucket-wheel?"

"What is the bucket-wheel?"

"That's the machine made of wood which is used to draw the water from the well for watering the gardens."

"I'll try."

"Well then, you draw one hundred buckets of water and I shall give you in return a glassful of milk."

"Very well."

Giangio led the puppet into the garden and taught him how to turn the bucket-wheel. Pinocchio set to work immediately, but before he had drawn the hundred buckets of water he was running with sweat from head to feet. He had never worked as hard as this before.

"Until now," said the farmer, "the work of turning the bucket-wheel was done by my donkey, but today that poor animal is near the end of his life."

"Could I please see him?"

"Certainly."

When Pinocchio was led into the stall he saw a pretty donkey stretched out on the straw, worn out from hunger and over-work. When he had looked at him closely he said to himself anxiously,

"I recognize this donkey! I have seen that face before!"

He leaned down close to him and asked him in the donkey dialect:

"Who are you?"

At this question the donkey opened its dying eyes and replied, mumbling in the same dialect,

"I am Lu-ci-gno-lo."

And he closed his eyes, put his head down, and died.

"Oh poor Lucignolo!" said Pinocchio in a soft voice, and he took a handful of straw and dried a tear that had run down his face.

"You are certainly very upset about a donkey that

166

has cost you nothing." said the farmer. "How much should I be upset? I paid hard cash for it!"

"Well, you see . . . He was a friend of mine!"

"A friend?"

"A schoolmate!"

"What!" cried Giangio giving a loud laugh. "What! You have some donkeys for schoolmates? I can guess what fine students they would make!"

The puppet was cut to the quick by these words, and did not answer. He took the glassful of milk which was still warm and returned home to the cottage.

From that day on, for more than five months, he left his bed every morning before dawn and went to turn the bucket-wheel. In that way he earnt the milk which was helping so much to improve the health of his father.

Nor was he content with this. As time went on he learnt also how to make baskets and trays out of reeds, and with the money that he earnt by selling them he managed, with a great amount of care, to meet the daily expenses. He also built by himself a very elegant little cart for taking his father for a walk.

He stayed up each evening and began to teach himself to read and write. He had bought in the near-by village, for a few cents, a large old book with some pages missing that he used as a reader. To practise writing he used a sharpened stick of straw as a pen, and because he had neither inkwell nor ink he dipped his pen in a little jar full of the syrup of blackberry juice.

His strong desire to learn and his efforts to improve himself made it possible for him to keep his sick father in reasonable comfort. He even managed to put aside some money to buy himself new clothes.

One morning he said to his father—

"I'm going to the market near by to buy myself a little jacket, a cap, and a pair of shoes. When I return home," he added laughing, "I shall be dressed so well that you'll mistake me for a great lord."

He went out of the house and began to run along very happy and pleased. Suddenly he heard himself called by name, and he turned to see a beautiful snail who was coming out of the hedge.

"Don't you recognize me?" asked the snail.

"I think, and yet. . . ."

"Don't you remember that snail who lived with the Fairy with the raven-coloured hair? Don't you recall that time when she came down to give you a light, and your foot was stuck in the door of the house?"

"I remember it all," cried Pinocchio. "Answer me quickly, my dear little snail, where have you left my good Fairy? What is she doing? Has she pardoned me? Does she think of me always? Does she still love me? Is she far from here? Can I go to meet her?"

All these questions were asked very hurriedly and without taking breath, but the snail replied with her usual slowness,

"My dear Pinocchio, the poor Fairy is lying in bed in hospital."

"In hospital?"

"Yes, unfortunately! She has suffered a thousand misfortunes and has become seriously ill. She has not been able to buy herself anything to eat."

"Really? Oh, how sad you have made me! Oh my poor Fairy! My poor little Fairy! My poor little Fairy! . . . If I had a million dollars I would run to give them to her, but I have only forty cents. Here they are. I was just going to buy myself a new outfit of clothes. Take them, snail, and give them at once to my good Fairy."

"What about your new clothes?"

"What do new clothes matter to me? I would sell these rags that I'm wearing if it would help. Go, snail, and hurry. In two days return here and I hope to be able to give you some more money. Up to now I have worked to keep my father. From today I will work five hours more to keep my good mother also. Goodbye, snail, and in two days I shall await you."

The snail, unlike her usual custom, began to run like a lizard in the hot days of midsummer.

When Pinocchio returned home his father asked him, "Where are the new clothes?"

"It wasn't possible to find any that suited me well. Never mind! I'll buy them another time."

That evening, Pinocchio, instead of staying up until ten, stayed up until midnight, and instead of making eight baskets of reeds, he made sixteen. Then he went to bed and slept.

When sleeping he seemed to see in a dream the Fairy, all beautiful and smiling, who kissed him and said, "Good boy, Pinocchio! In reward for the goodness of your heart I excuse you for all the mischief that you have done up until today. Boys who love and help their parents who are poor and sick, as you have, deserve a great deal of praise, even if they have not always been models of obedience and good conduct. Be just as thoughful in the future, and you will be happy."

At this point the dream finished and Pinocchio awoke.

You can imagine his feeling of wonder when he became aware that he was no longer a puppet of wood; he had become a real boy like all the others. He looked all round, and instead of the straw walls of the cottage, he saw a fine room, furnished and decorated very pleasantly. He jumped out of bed and found ready for him a beautiful new outfit of clothes, a new cap, and a new pair of leather boots which shone like a mirror.

He was no sooner dressed than he put his hand in his pocket and took out a little ivory box on which these words were written:

THE FAIRY WITH THE RAVEN-COLOURED HAIR RETURNS TO HER DEAR PINOCCHIO THE FORTY CENTS AND THANKS HIM VERY MUCH FOR HIS GOOD HEART.

He opened the box, and instead of the copper coins that he had given, the same number of gold coins shone there brightly, all new from the mint.

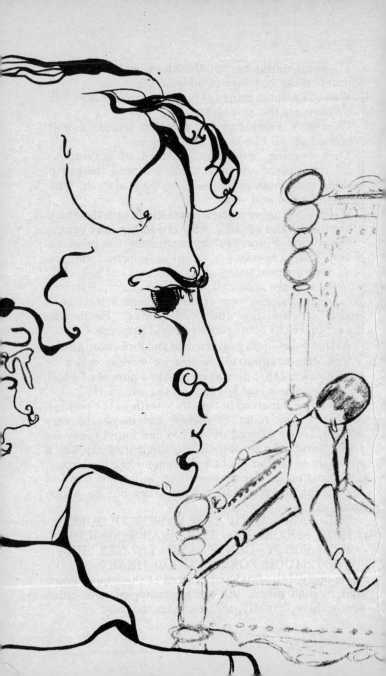

He went to look in the mirror and seemed to see another person. He no longer saw the usual reflection of a wooden puppet; he saw the bright and intelligent face of a handsome boy with chestnut-coloured hair, shining eyes, and a happy, joyful smile.

In the midst of all these wonders, which came quickly one after the other, Pinocchio did not know if he was really awake or if he was dreaming with his eyes open.

"Where's my father?" he called out suddenly, and just then he went into the room next door and found old Geppetto, now healthy, bright and cheerful, as he had been long ago. He was working again at his trade of woodcarving. He was now designing a beautiful ornament of wood, rich with leaves and flowers.

"Please satisfy my curiosity, my dear father. How did this sudden change come about?" Pinocchio asked, running up to him and embracing his neck and covering him with kisses.

"This sudden change in our house was brought about because you deserved it," said Geppetto.

"Why did I deserve it?"

"Because when boys who have been bad become good, they can create a new and happy feeling within their own families."

"And where is the old Pinocchio of wood hidden away?"

"There he is," answered Geppetto and he nodded towards a large puppet lying in a chair with its head hanging on one side, its arms dangling and its legs crossed. It was folded in half so that it seemed to stay upright only by a miracle.

Pinocchio turned and looked at it, and after a time he said to himself with a great sense of satisfaction,

"How funny I looked as a puppet, and how good it is to be a real boy!"